A
DEVELOPING COUNTRY

B David Peck

abbott press

Copyright © 2013, 2015 B David Peck.

All rights reserved. No part of this book may be used or reproduced by any means, graphic, electronic, or mechanical, including photocopying, recording, taping or by any information storage retrieval system without the written permission of the publisher except in the case of brief quotations embodied in critical articles and reviews.

Abbott Press books may be ordered through booksellers or by contacting:

Abbott Press
1663 Liberty Drive
Bloomington, IN 47403
www.abbottpress.com
Phone: 1-866-697-5310

Because of the dynamic nature of the Internet, any web addresses or links contained in this book may have changed since publication and may no longer be valid. The views expressed in this work are solely those of the author and do not necessarily reflect the views of the publisher, and the publisher hereby disclaims any responsibility for them.

Any people depicted in stock imagery provided by Thinkstock are models, and such images are being used for illustrative purposes only. Certain stock imagery © Thinkstock.

ISBN: 978-1-4582-0633-6 (sc)
ISBN: 978-1-4582-0635-0 (hc)
ISBN: 978-1-4582-0634-3 (e)

Library of Congress Control Number: 2013906905

Print information available on the last page.

Abbott Press rev. date: 7/31/15

CHAPTER 1

The packed classroom at the historic black college came to hear Ruth Mitchell discuss her contemporary civilization course. As she finished explaining the assignments and described the great books they would be reading, a white man stood, raised his hand and then sat down.

Ruth pointed to him and said, "My husband Joshua is reminding me that we must leave soon." She looked at a clock on the wall. "We have time for a few questions."

A girl on the front row began, "Mrs. Mitchell when the school year ends, you famously disappear and nobody can contact you. Rumor has it that you discovered a utopia. If we swear to keep it a secret and not to call you, will you tell us about your beautiful hiding place?"

The beloved teacher joined in the laughter. "Joshua is an advisor to a developing country in southeast Africa, next to Mozambique, called Bessedelya. It is not as beautiful as our Virginia, and unless you enjoy traffic jams, high taxes and earthquakes, I don't think you would call Bessedelya a utopia."

A Developing Country

"What then is the attraction?" asked a boy in the back.

"Living day and night without fear of violence. An honor system that has to be experienced. Imagine doors left unlocked or going back to the park days after you misplaced something and finding it where you left it. I love the friendliness, the optimism. It reminds me of small town America in the sixties."

"I assume most of the people are black," said a boy on the aisle. "How are they different from us?"

Joshua was helping Ruth put on her coat when she asked him, "How are they different?"

Joshua hesitated to criticize his wife's admirers, but then said, "America's young people are more cynical than the people there. You're too smart to be fooled, probably because you never believed in anything in the first place. You say our justice system is racist. Our economy perpetuates privilege. Our institutions are tools of the power elite. Our founders were hypocrites." Joshua looked at the audience and then asked, "If almost every person of color you'd meet there would tell you that he loves his country, would you agree that Bessedelyans are different?"

"Maybe they don't have a memory of the injustices and humiliations we suffered," said a voice in the back. "When I look in the mirror, I see a man with the wrong color. I know I won't be treated the same as you."

"They definitely see themselves differently than you do," Joshua said. "They love their blackness. Although everyone is taught Africa's terrible history, they don't look back in anger. They are not still shackled to the past."

As Ruth and Joshua walked to the door someone asked," So what is this developing country developing?"

"Much the same as we're doing here," Ruth said. "Maybe a few more visionaries."

CHAPTER 2

Not far from the college, a distinguished African American, Jakob Warsaw, worked his way through the morning crowd at Washington's Union station. At the exit near the taxi stand, he put down his two brief cases, found a seat and took a pad from his jacket. As he began to write, a white man knocked a suitcase against his leg, stared at him and kept running.

Jake looked at a black girl seated nearby. She was wearing a cap facing backwards with the letters MCV. When he saw the Medical College of Virginia sticker on the suitcase, he placed it next to her diaper bag. She was turned away from him, had finished breast feeding and was putting her baby in a sling. It looked to Jake as though she were struggling and he asked, "Can I help you?"

Hinda Raisal laughed, "He was hungry. I don't think you have the right equipment but thanks."

"Taking a Christmas break?" Jake asked.

"On my way home, to Africa," Hinda explained. "I just finished my residency."

"Congratulations," Jake said.

Hinda stood, rocked her baby and sat down.

"From Africa," Jake mused, "and you chose a school in Richmond. May I ask why?"

"My country will pay for graduate study anywhere. They want me to head a new health and education ministry," Hinda explained. "I have more interest in American history than in medicine."

"I don't follow you," Jake said.

"I wanted to know how a few men could have created this amazing country," Hinda said. "Where better than Virginia to learn about the Founders? My dream is to live to see a United States of Africa."

"You'll have to live a long time," said Jake.

"You look like a lawyer," she said. "I bet you could help us solve some start-up problems."

"I can't help myself stop smoking," Jake said.

"You're being modest," Hinda said. "I bet you are on your way to persuade a jury that your client did not mean to defraud those people, and he's really sorry they were evicted from their homes."

"You're close," said Jake. "I'm on my way to a hearing where I'll try to explain the unintended consequences of an earmark that benefits one company. The few Senators that show up will be more concerned with the CSPAN cameras than with my brilliant comments."

"Are you kidding me?" asked Hinda. "You're going to testify before the most powerful men in Washington?"

"That would be the lobbyists," Jake corrected.

He looked at his watch, took a business card from his wallet and while writing said, "Joshua Mitchell, our managing partner, has a client who also wants to see a United States of Africa. Gadhafi is a madman, but he gives big money to dreamers like you. Contact JM. He may be able to help you meet the Colonel."

Jake handed her the business card and picked up his brief cases. "Good luck doctor," he said and hurried to the exit.

Hinda put the card in her jacket, gathered her luggage and walked outside to the line waiting for the taxis. She did not notice the card drop from her pocket when she told the driver to take her to the airport.

CHAPTER
3

Fifteen Years Later

Traffic at the industrial waterfront had come to a stop. When Angel the limousine driver left to see what had happened, his passenger was watching a container crane lifting a box onto a ship.

Jake was reminded of the summer he worked as a rigger loading trucks and railroad cars. It was strenuous and often dangerous work, but he loved the sights and sounds of the huge equipment and the spirit of the operators and laborers.

During the past year, the continuing and deserved criticism of the world of finance had made the days much less enjoyable. Seeing longshoremen and teamsters at work reminded Jake of happier times.

Angel knocked the snow from his shoes when he returned and pointed to the car in front of them. "I just looked in that van, a bunch of black guys. One kid was putting on his hat." Angel lifted his hands to his head. "He had on handcuffs. Those dudes are going to jail."

Jake leaned forward to see what the driver was talking about. Picturing the handcuffed boy with the hat, his fingers touched the fedora on the seat. For a moment the fifty-two-year-old man was afraid of the criminals in the van. He reached a button that locked all the doors, sat back and opened his newspaper.

"You know what I think, Mr. Warner?" Angel asked. "At school they hear their families were brought here as slaves and treated like animals. On the street they smoke some weed and are locked up with a bunch of angry, sick bastards. It's no wonder some good kids go to the bad."

"What's the solution?" Jake asked.

"Suppose they grew up in a city with all black people. You know, black police, black judges, black businesses, black leaders. I bet they wouldn't be on their way to prison."

"You and Marcus Garvey," Jake said.

"Say what?"

"Africa has many cities like that."

"So what do you think, Mr. Warner?"

"My name is Warsaw."

The traffic started moving. Suddenly, towering over the old warehouses, the flight deck of an aircraft carrier appeared.

The GPS voice said they had reached their destination as Angel pulled up to the gate of a scrap metal operation. A guard checked their identification, called someone on his cell phone and then pointed to a small grey building in front of two ships tied to a finger pier.

A Developing Country

Angel drove past several mountains of metal to a parking area as three people approached the car. One was a short, fat man wearing a blue hardhat and smoking a cigarette. He was followed by a well-dressed man and a voluptuous woman wearing yellow visitor hardhats.

As Jake got out of the car, the man with the yellow hat extended his hand. "Mr. Warsaw, I'm attorney Allan Stone. It's an honor to meet you."

"The pleasure is mine, Mr. Stone."

The lawyer chuckled nervously. "That's very gracious sir, but you're the Washington legend. I simply represent the detainees. Mr. Johnson here owns the shipyard. Miss Maybey is from the Justice Department. We were told to contact you if there were any important problems."

Johnson shook Jake's hand, handed him a yellow hardhat and motioned for everyone to follow him to the carrier. Halfway down the pier, stairs on a scaffold rose twenty feet in the air alongside the great ship. At the top of the stairs they crossed a gangplank into a cavernous area under the flight deck and then followed Johnson through a passage into a large room.

Thirty men were standing or sitting by several long tables. They wore red uniforms marked with the white letters POW. Some wore leg irons. They were guarded by five military policemen.

Stone began to make his case. "Taking men captured in Iraq to Guantánamo prison was not a good idea. The president inherited the problem and we know he asked you to fix it, but incarceration on a ship would never have satisfied the courts or public opinion."

Jake knew that JM, urged by the previous president to handle this controversial problem, had then asked Jake to find a place for the prisoners until they could be brought to trial.

8

He thought about the young associate in their firm who had come up with the ship prison idea. She persuaded the others that this plan would temporarily solve the government's legal problem of detainment. He could not imagine trying to explain her reasoning to Mr. Stone.

"Is that why it was urgent for me to be here today?" Jake asked.

"I would have called you sooner," Stone said, "but I was just able to arrange my schedule to meet with my clients. It's not at all clear that these people, who've never been charged and never had a day in court, are prisoners of war. And if not, that POW designation is misleading and demeaning. Several of the men complained about seasickness, and the clothes are not warm enough. The Geneva Conventions are very clear."

Jake turned to Mr. Johnson. "Are you having a problem with this arrangement?"

Johnson averted his eyes clearly uncomfortable with this discussion. "My employees hate having dangerous men in the plant, men who might have killed American soldiers, and I'm not too happy keeping them here myself."

"But you are paid a lot of money for your discomfort, aren't you Mr. Johnson?" Jake asked.

Johnson colored slightly. "I'm not saying it's not," he said, "but more important to me, I'm doing something for the country. The governor called me himself to say I was performing a great service."

"You're a patriot and having our enemies here bothers you, is that it?" asked Jake.

"Not just that. You see those cranes loading that steel and those railroad cars being moved by that switching engine? When the MPs bring these men out for a break, they don't listen to the guards. They'll stop on the tracks and watch, or drop down and pray. Don't get me wrong. I don't care if they get hit by falling scrap or run over by the trucks. I'm afraid I'll get sued by Mr. Stone or get fined for a safety violation if they get hurt. I was told I'm getting paid to provide a place until the government figures out what to do with these people."

Jake concluded that Johnson was satisfied with the money but afraid of lawsuits. Stone was happy with the potential of years of legal work and wanted some idea of how the government intended to defend its action. The Justice Department lady had not expressed an opinion, but she was a beautiful sight shivering in the cold.

Jake had a plane to catch. He turned to Ms. Maybey and said, "Send them back to Guantánamo as soon as possible."

Maybey looked shocked. "What? It took us months to get these arrangements approved. Your governor and senators took a lot of heat. You've got to give us more time."

Jake shook his head.

When Jake returned to the limousine, the driver was sitting in the backseat. He had been watching the news on the car's television set. "This guy hurt a lot of people," Angel said as he climbed out of the car and got behind the wheel. "They said he won't serve time and he showed no remorse. What's that mean, *no remorse?*"

"He didn't say he was sorry," Jake said.

"It don't seem fair," Angel said. "People struggle to take care of their families. They play by the rules. A guy they trust loses their money, and he's not even sorry. In my opinion they should just kill the son of a bitch."

"Will the people get their money back after they kill him?" Jake asked.

"Maybe not, but while trying to make their payments, they'll know he won't hurt nobody else," Angel said.

Jake knew many men like the one Angel was talking about. Admired in their communities, all were oblivious of the damage they inflicted on innocent people. There was no punishment for those animals.

"We don't kill people for nonviolent crimes."

Approaching the airport, Angel nearly missed the entrance to the departure area, swerved and skidded on the snow. "Sorry Mr. Warner."

Jake fumbled to answer his cell phone and heard JM's gruff voice.

"I just heard from Ed Gutierrez. He said there's going to be a top resignation at Treasury. His people think you should go for it. They want to know whether to float your name."

Jake was pleased. He had often thought of a cabinet position. "What do you think?"

"A once-in-a-lifetime opportunity. You want to talk about it later?" JM asked.

"I'm on my way to the forum in Davos," Jake said. "Tell Eddie I'll call him tomorrow."

After Jake disconnected the call, he thought about the prisoners. The associate in his firm had explained that during World War II, German POWs were brought to the states. If we could put them to work in another country, it should provide a temporary solution. He called his secretary and asked her to get Jerry Goodman in Jerusalem on the phone.

A Developing Country

Angel pulled up to the curb between two shuttle buses and went to the trunk to get the luggage.

Jake waved to a familiar baggage porter as his office connected his call to Israel.

Goodman's wife answered.

"Maggie, it's Jake. Sorry to call so late. I hope you're all well."

"We're good. You're inviting us to your wedding to the TV reporter?" she asked.

"You've got me confused with somebody in love. But speaking of marriages, I don't want to start any rumors, but I hear your husband has been fooling around. It's time to trade in the old goat for two thirty-year-olds."

"What would I do with them? Stay well, Jakob. Let me get Jerry."

Jerry was on the phone. "Is everything all right?"

"I'm fine," Jake said. "Do you still work with the king's brother in Jordan? I could use his help."

"I was with him yesterday," Jerry said.

"Ask him to find me twenty acres at the Gulf of Aqaba," Jake said. "It has to have access to deep water. I want to bring in damaged equipment and junk from the Iraq war, cut it up and ship it to India. I'm trying to make work for about thirty prisoners from Guantánamo. If it looks like we can get the property, I'll get you more information."

CHAPTER 4

The World Economic Forum in Davos was unusually well attended. The terrible recession and market crash had caused havoc in many countries. Protesters filled the streets. In Greece, Spain, Ireland, Italy and other Western countries, the ruling governments had been replaced or were threatened to be overturned. Leaders from all over the world had come to hear suggestions and solutions from men and women who had instituted programs that worked or from economists whose ideas had not been discredited.

At the conclusion of a military weapons proliferation panel discussion, Jake and two French friends joined the crowd at the elevators.

Marcel said to Jake, "So because your parents gave you away as a baby, you have had nothing to do with your African birthplace, no curiosity about their reasons. Maybe you were too ugly to keep."

Pierre had a different explanation. "Perhaps you were bartered for things they valued more like a roll of toilet paper."

"No interest in meeting relatives?" asked Marcel. "Ever consider the business opportunity missed? Suppose one of your cousins is the head of Africa's drug trade?"

The three of them entered the elevator.

Pierre asked, "Before anyone could be in the president's cabinet, he must have a deep background check, yes?"

"If I came to America as an infant, how could I be a security risk?" Jake asked.

"You've never heard of a sleeper cell?" Pierre asked. "I happen to know Osama Ben Laden's mother's maiden name was similar to Warsaw. You my friend may be related to the world's most feared terrorist by injection."

The three men were laughing when they left the elevator.

Dr. Hinda Raisal, one of the speakers, had begun to make a name for herself for several extraordinary accomplishments in the little known country Bessedelya. Her decisive but controversial actions had stopped an Ebola outbreak and controlled the spread of sexually transmitted diseases. She was credited for a courageous confrontation with the generals that averted a military coup, and she had begun meeting the continent's leaders with the ultimate goal of creating a united Africa.

The beautiful black woman was standing in an alcove of the busy lobby making changes to her remarks when a woman with a clipboard stopped in front of her.

"Dr. Raisal? I finally found you," she said.

"Is something wrong?" Hinda asked.

"Nothing serious. I have you on the HIV/aids panel, yes?" the German lady asked.

"No. I'm malaria," Hinda said.

"Good. They have changed your room to the Zurich on the third floor." She smiled and left.

Hinda looked up from her work and noticed two white men and a black man staring at her. One walked over and read her badge.

"Dr. Raisal perhaps you can help me," Marcel said in French.

"Yes?"

The Frenchman had a broad smile. "Every meeting I've attended described a worsening financial disaster. Could you prescribe an antidepressant?"

Hinda, angered by the interruption, saw Jake try to pull away his friend. She glared at the black "Frenchman."

She asked, "Do you speak English?"

"A little," Jake replied.

"Please leave me the fuck alone," Hinda said.

Jake saw that she had a speaker tag. He said, "I want to apologize for my friend." Hinda wore a look of disgust. Jake continued, "Don't be so tough. I'm sorry he bothered you. I'd like to hear what you have to say. I'm sure it will be more interesting than what I was going to hear."

"It would put you to sleep," she said.

"I hope so," Jake said. "I didn't get much last night."

"One thirty. The Zurich room."

All the seats were filled and people were standing in the back when Jake finally arrived.

A Developing Country

Hinda was concluding her talk. "I did not come with a begging bowl," she was saying. "For too many years and in too many ways, Africa has given its wealth to you. You built your countries with people and natural resources ripped from our families and our land. It's time to repay your enormous debt to us. I have tried to tell you what is needed and what actions you should take. Please let me know you will be with us in this terrible fight."

The audience rose to its feet and applauded. Some tearful spectators rushed to embrace Hinda. When she was finally free of the many well-wishers, she walked over to Jake.

"Impressive presentation Doctor," he said. "As far as I could see, you kept everyone awake."

"But did they hear what I was saying? Will they be moved to act?" Hinda asked.

Although he heard little of her talk, Jake was impressed by the intensity of her feelings. He was not familiar with anyone so passionately concerned about humanity. In his world, it was all about power and money. He realized his usual cynical response would not be appreciated.

"Can we talk more about it over a drink?" was all Jake could manage.

"I've got to pack," Hinda said and then paused. "Sure, why not?"

As they walked to the barroom Jake said, "Do you really expect to make a difference? Malaria has been around forever."

"You hope to reach someone. Somebody the leaders will listen to," she replied, "maybe the person who must solve the problem. I want him to know what worked for me in my country." Hesitating to continue her lecture, she read his name tag. "What do you do, Jakob Warsaw?"

"I'm a consultant. I'm called when cities or countries have special situations usually financial problems."

"A consultant. You interview everybody, summarize their comments and package their ideas in a binder. Actually you don't really do anything do you?" Hinda smiled.

"Maybe I can do something for you," offered Jake, "a free consultation, only not about malaria."

"We take many immigrants, refugees, slaves that we buy and set free," said Hinda. "They must be taught English. We don't have enough teachers or classrooms, and they work in jobs all over the country. They must learn to respect our institutions and that certain behavior is not acceptable."

"Two different problems," said Jake. "Illiterate people were a challenge for the Church a thousand years ago. Very few people were able to read or write, but they could listen to sermons. They could hear homilies explained at the Sunday services. You could provide the immigrants DVD players. Families could sit together watching teachers lecture in their native language. They could listen to CDs on their way to and from work."

"Interesting," Hinda said. "What about their behavior? They resist our laws. We treat women much differently than they do."

"A much more complicated problem than teaching English," said Jake. "But I think we can solve it at supper. What time and where can I meet you?"

"Consultants I've seen," said Hinda ignoring his offer, "are more interested in preserving their jobs than speaking truth to power. Referring problems to committees is too often the recommendation."

"That's a little harsh," said Jake. "We wouldn't be called if we didn't help the people understand their options."

"When principles are at stake, I think advisors should vote with their feet. Sitting silently must be considered agreement."

"Walking out would be too dramatic for me," Jake said. "If my best efforts don't persuade the client, I move on."

"I can't move on. I have to stay until the problem is under control."

"What happens when there's uncertainty about the facts and there are no good options? The decider says, 'I need your advice tonight.' What do you do then?"

"I pick up a stranger. Get him to take me to a bar." She laughed and lifted her glass. "I really must go. Thanks for the drink. Au revoir."

Jake was surprised by his strong attraction to this woman. Hinda was pretty, but he knew a lot of beautiful women. As she walked away, he saw her look back at him, smile and disappear into the crowded lobby.

Hinda, back in her room, kicked off her shoes. She was impressed with the handsome American. Was he late forties, early fifties? She took off her belt, skirt and blouse. As she washed her face, she admired her figure in the full-length mirror. She put her suitcase on a luggage rack and then sat on the bed.

At the thought that his wife was short and fat, she smiled, lay back and closed her eyes. She imagined Jakob touching her and felt his fingers inside her. She moaned as she came and then fell asleep.

CHAPTER 5

A few days later, Jake was back in his Richmond office. Men and women filled the glass-enclosed rooms staring at computers. Important business was conducted here.

Jake and JM were quiet as they walked past Jake's secretary seated outside his office. On the phone, Kay nodded to the two men as an excited intern approached her desk with a note.

The young staffer could not wait to tell her, "It's from *Air Force One*. The president's chief of staff wants Mr. Warsaw to call as soon as possible."

On the bookshelves and paneled walls inside Jake's office were a number of awards and pictures of him in different settings. In one he was playing the piano with a small group in a smoke-filled room. In another, dressed in his fencing uniform, he was receiving a bronze medal at the Olympics. Several pictures showed Jake with world-renowned leaders. In most of the pictures he was the only black person.

Kay walked in with a carafe of water, a bottle of pills and a stack of mail. Jake noticed her wiping her eyes.

"Are you crying?" he asked.

"My lawyer just told me I can't make her leave my house," Kay cried. "I bought it. I pay the mortgage. He said I may have to pay her alimony."

Jake was thoughtful. He looked at JM and then at Kay. "Suppose I bought the house? I'd evict her, change the locks and sell the house back to you for a dollar more than I paid. Ask your lawyer if that will work."

"Oh my God, the bitch will go crazy!" Kay yelled. She hugged Jake.

"Get out of here," he said, pushing her away. "She should get the house for putting up with you."

She handed him his messages and a package. "The White House is furious about the prisoners on the ship, and Mr. Mitchell, Senator Daniel called. He said to remind you that you were going to offer a suggestion about something he mailed you, more coffee anyone?" Kay walked toward the door.

Mitchell shook his head. "The State Department wants us to find ten million dollars for an African general. What's the name of his country just north of Gabon? I can't remember shit. They need his vote at the UN."

Jake had started to open a manila envelope. "What if we send them some government surplus assets, obsolete tanks, planes? The metal, the equipment, even the fuel will be worth more money than they're asking for. And the jobs, the general could put hundreds of people to work."

When he removed a letter from the envelope, a blue bottle and a yellowed photograph fell out.

JM was dismissive of Jake's idea. "The country is his family business. The money he wants goes to his personal bank account. I don't think the Swiss have begun accepting old tanks from their depositors. Besides, the bastard couldn't care less about jobs."

Jake ignored JM and laughed when he read the letter. "Can you believe they just found this stuff at my first foster home, from an old file cabinet?"

"I guess they go through their records every fifty years whether they need to or not," JM said.

Jake put the bottle on his desk, looked at the faded picture and handed it to JM. Nine black men, women and children were smiling at the camera. The crease, where the photo had been folded, obscured the face of a man next to a pregnant woman.

"Recognize any of these people?" JM asked.

Jake shook his head, "Must be friends of the missionaries who left me there. I was an infant." He crushed the unwanted mail into a ball and shot it toward the trash can. He put the blue bottle on the corner of his desk and looked at JM. "I'm trying to remember when you told me you were leaving."

"I told Ruth I'd pick her up in two hours. Traffic will be terrible. You want to go to the gala with us?"

"I mean to Africa. When is your port meeting? What is your itinerary?"

"We go to Rome on the tenth. Ruth will wait for me there. No direct flights to Bessedelya. You have to stop at the Fun City resort. After the hearing, maybe two days, I'll meet her back in Rome."

Jake said, "I'm thinking about going."

"To Bessedelya? You've never wanted to talk about that country."

"Until now," he explained. "If I spend a day or two, I may be able to get answers to questions about the people who sold me."

"You're right," JM said. "Everything about the next secretary of the Treasury is going to be in the media. You don't want to see a little girl on TV pointing to your picture saying, 'He forced me to play hide the wiener.'"

"I'm not worried about anything like that. For the first time in my life, I'm having dreams about Africa. Last night, I saw a woman in a dashiki. She was standing with a baby on the porch of a small house. People had gathered in the rain to listen to her sing. She gave the child to a white man."

"I don't do dreams."

"A week ago I had a nightmare in which I saw people searching for that baby. They were calling for me."

"Get an unlisted number. Better yet, call a psychiatrist."

"Do you think they may help me find the people who gave me away?" Jake asked.

"I'm sure of it. Their information systems are state of the art. It's the most modern country in Africa," JM said. "And Jake you may be the one most responsible for its creation."

Although it took place many years ago, Jake recalled his nervousness when told that managing partner Mitchell wanted him at his meeting in New York, and the African group's surprise when the expert called in was a young black man with glasses and an Afro.

"I was so new to the firm," Jake said. "I never dreamed you'd have me working on such a big deal much less my birthplace."

"We were stuck," JM said. "Their advisors couldn't understand that no banks and few lenders were interested in a startup country. The group we brought to the table was ready to walk until you figured out how to make it work."

"And I almost got you fired."

"No you made me look good. More important, we made a lot of money on the deal. Everything was perfect until you took the leader's kid to Greenwich Village."

"I never hurt her," Jake protested. "We had some bad dope. I think we both hallucinated, but I never hurt her."

"You went meshuga."

"I remember I couldn't stop laughing. I was amazed to be in bed with one of the delegation's daughters celebrating her new country. Then it hit me, the rage. It was where I was born. What kind of parents would give away their baby? I just lost it."

"Thank God our work was done the next day."

"She was so beautiful. Whatever happened to her?"

JM was pensive. "She died in a car accident. It must be thirty-five years ago. I think she left a little girl."

CHAPTER
6

In Bessedelya, the presidential residence was a former army barracks. The few furnishings in the building were modest and well-worn. In the president's bedroom, a floor fan blew the simple curtains on the screened windows.

Hinda Raisal saw a strange look on President Simba's face. The eighty-five-year-old man looked embarrassed.

"What's the matter Papa?"

"Peed in my pants," the president said.

Hinda picked up a telephone. "Tell Mkeeba that the president needs some help. Well, tell him to finish what he's doing and get up here."

The president read his newspaper. "Suicide Bomber Kills Eight on School Bus. Who would do something like this? What do these people want?"

"We don't know yet. Some Islamic group claimed responsibility," Hinda said. "Ali said.."

"Who's Ali?"

"Your vice president," Hinda said.

"Isn't he Islamic?"

"He told me he's never heard of this group."

"Then why? I'm so confused."

Hinda put her arm around his shoulder. "You'll be all right."

"When is the election? Don't I have some meetings?" he asked.

"You're not well enough for this campaign. You'll sit out this election. Ali will take your place until you're better."

"How is he doing?"

"It's close, but he's leading."

"Who is he leading?" he asked.

"William Gee's son BG."

"My friend William, he's a good man."

"His son Billigee."

"Smart boy. Went to school in the states," he said. "Okay I'll see you at supper."

"No. I'll be away for a few days, in Copenhagen."

"What's there?"

"A World Health Organization meeting. I'm one of the speakers."

"I just saw you on the television, giving a speech."

"That was last month in Paris," she said.

"Always running. These trips any good? Do you meet people who can help us?"

"Sometimes."

Mkeeba, the president's bodyguard, entered the room and waved for Hinda to leave. As he began to undress the president, she closed the door, looked at the messages on her cell phone and placed a call to her son.

"This is mom," said Hinda.

"How can the TV news talk about a death penalty?" Stephen asked.

"I can't understand you Stephen," said Hinda. "Stop crying."

"He's like my brother and my best friend."

"It's the punishment for the pain he caused his girlfriend and her family."

"They know it was an accident."

"And they know she will be crippled for the rest of her life. The law doesn't give a judge much discretion. He was the driver of the car."

"What can I do?"

"Stay next to him, at his house, with his family until the appeal."

"I can't stop crying."

"I'm sad too."

When Mkeeba left, Hinda returned to the room and began to adjust the president's tie.

"William Gee and me go way back," he explained.

Hinda had heard the story many times. "You told me, Papa."

"His wife drove a dump truck," he continued. "When her mining company boss made her pregnant, she stole the truck and married William. He said they hardly knew each other. She'd only spoke to him a few times. They drove her truck to Bessedelya. We met at the fights. He was a barber. When he cut my hair, I told him about all the things we were building. He told her, and she borrowed money and bought another truck. Now they're rich. But you know William still cuts my hair for free."

"That's nice," she said. Hinda looked at two walls of the bedroom that were covered with pictures. "Do you remember my mother?"

He shook his head. Everybody sent him pictures. He forgot their names a long time ago, and he stopped apologizing for not going to the baptisms, weddings, funerals, confirmations and birthday parties. Hinda was always his favorite. He loved the way she took charge and handled so many of his problems. "I remember you," he said, "leading the other children around, real bossy, big glasses. Men don't like bossy women."

"I had boyfriends," Hinda said.

"Always reading books," he said. "No bosoms and your ass was too little."

Hinda took a pillow from the bed. "They sell padding for your butt and your boobs."

"You're too smart for the men. Do you have somebody for sex, or do you have to do yourself?"

"You know your car is missing a hubcap. The president should not drive a car without a hubcap."

CHAPTER 7

Outside Jake's office, his white ex-wife Nancy and their grandchild Liz appeared. Kay was glad to see her.

"You look fabulous," Kay said as she hugged Nancy.

"Your new security guard, he's fabulous. What a pair of buns." She used her umbrella to scan Kay's body. "And when he waved that wand over my breasts, I almost beeped." Nancy laughed.

"He's married," Kay said.

"So am I." Nancy nodded toward Jake's office. "Is he busy?"

Kay shook her head, picked up a jug of liquid from the floor and led the two visitors into Jake's office. JM stood to hug Nancy, and Liz greeted her grandfather.

"They sent over this stuff to drink the night before your colonoscopy," Kay told Jake putting the jug next to his desk.

"It's nothing," Jake explained to the worried looks. "I had some bleeding."

Nancy handed Jake some receipts. "We were shopping. I ordered a few gifts. I knew you'd want to get something for our daughter. You know her party is.."

"Jesus Christ, Nancy." He looked at the extravagant purchases. "Your husband is supposed to be loaded."

"He doesn't give me money for *our* children," she answered. She sat next to JM and began whispering to him.

After several trips around the room, the little girl accidentally knocked the blue bottle and photo from the desk.

"Lizzy!" Nancy left JM and picked up the picture and the cracked bottle.

Kay came in with a drink for Nancy, saw the incident and put her arm around the little girl. "Come with me," she said. "I've got something to show you."

Nancy held up the blue bottle. "Nice perfume. Are you dating someone from a trailer park?" and then she looked at the photo with the nine Africans. "This picture reminds me. You know the references we sent for Lizzy? Not enough. They want more background information on her relatives."

"So do I. Tell them to check Slave.com," Jake said.

Nancy gave an air kiss to JM and left.

"She just gave me some bad news," JM said. "Last summer she let some people use your farm. A few days ago she was told that hazardous material was found in the ground water and running off into that stream that meanders by the property. A lot of drums of chemicals were uncovered. You may not have enough money to clean up that mess."

CHAPTER 8

There were **banks of snow** and icy patches along the dark Virginia highway. Jake, dressed in his tuxedo, was running late for the gala at the Jefferson. He sped past the many slow drivers.

Jake was talking on his cell phone when he noticed red blinking lights in his rearview mirror. "I'm working on something Governor."

He pulled off the road, turned off his motor and watched the state trooper approach his car.

"Goddammit Jake," the governor said. "I told the White House weeks ago that you'd taken care of their problem. I need their help with a big contributor. What am I supposed to tell them when they call?"

The trooper approached and said, "Stay in your car. Let me see your license and registration."

"I'm sure we'll have something in a few days," Jake told the governor. "Can you hold on for a minute?" The governor said, "yes".

As he fumbled for the papers in his glove compartment, Jake remembered his last speeding ticket years ago. He recalled being terrified when a sheriff from a small Virginia town had stopped him. He told Jake to follow him, and Jake never forgot his fear during the interminable drive down narrow country roads until they arrived at the home of a justice of the peace where he paid a fine.

He was not frightened now as he handed the documents and the phone to the trooper. "Tell your boss what I did wrong."

CHAPTER 9

Jake pulled up to the entrance of the venerable Jefferson Hotel and gave his keys to the valet. He observed an unusual number of policemen and policewomen. A bellhop took his luggage to the front desk passing several secret servicemen wearing sunglasses and earphones. The lobby was crowded with gowned women and men dressed in formalwear. A large poster described the grand event, a benefit to fund the Slave Museum and grounds. The guest of honor was the vice president of the United States.

As he registered, Jake was ignored by everyone except for two people from the media.

"Mr. Warsaw," said Sally Raymond. "I'm with the *Washington Post*. May I ask you a few questions?"

"Sure," Jake said. He followed her and another reporter to a corner of the lobby.

"Has the president offered you the Treasury position?" she asked.

"No."

"Fred Holberg *New York Times*," said the black reporter. "This administration has the different faces of the United Nations, but the insiders look like they came from the same all-white fraternity. If you join that group, do you really think your voice will be heard?"

"I don't think they need me for window dressing," Jake said.

Ms. Raymond said, "It's been reported that you have a five million dollar income. Should we expect someone from your background to empathize with the millions who have lost their homes?"

Jake said, "Absolutely. If given the responsibility and authority, I will help them or resign."

"You've been conspicuously absent from discussions in the media on race-related issues," Holberg said. "Can we expect to hear you speak up in the future?"

"When I'm asked my opinion, the subject is usually about globalization or debt repayment," Jake said.

"Do you see yourself as a concerned African American?" Holberg asked.

"I see myself as an American," Jake said. He had had enough of the two reporters.

"Ask the people who see your picture," Holberg said. "They'll tell you who you are."

The staircase going down to the grand ballroom was reputed to have been used in the movie *Gone with the Wind*. As Jake descended, he was struck by the spectacular scene.

A Developing Country

Tables were laden with beautiful displays of food and flowers. Crowds formed around the several bars, and many people stood in the buffet lines. The dance floor was filled.

An attractive and popular TV reporter, Becky Allman, waved to Jake. She was surrounded by an admiring group. She mouthed, "Go. I'll find you."

Jake pointed to a far corner where he had seen JM and his wife and then made his way to a bar.

A short man stopped him and put his arm around Jake's waist. "One day my tennis partner here will lead a country," he announced to everyone nearby. "I'm telling you, he's got the right stuff. His ancestors were great leaders."

"How great were they?" someone asked.

"I promised to keep his secret, but I think I can trust you. He was born in an African country called *F'Gar wee*."

"I never heard of it," a woman at the bar said.

"His father was the head spear chucker of this dangerous place," the short man said.

"How dangerous was it?" someone asked.

"Every day they were threatened and had to fight for their lives. Every day the leader moved them to a new location, and then he'd drink himself to sleep," the short man said. "When he awoke in the morning his first words were so famous, they named the country for them."

"Don't ask him what the words were," someone pleaded, but the story teller continued.

"He would stand before his tribe, his hands outstretched and ask, 'Where the fuck are we?'"

Ruth saw Jake shake his head, take his drink and make his way through the crowd to her table.

She was playing with several children. "And I fought the Indians as hard as I could, but they scalped me anyway," Ruth said. When she removed her wig, the children laughed and screamed and fled to their parents.

Ruth's sense of humor put people at ease, and their laughter took her mind off her painful illness. Few appreciated her daily ordeal.

On the way to this gala, while JM was holding open the car door, she lost control of her bowels, messed up her clothes and went back inside to change.

While cleaning herself in the bathroom, her daughter called and immediately began describing the bad day she was having. "Can you believe my new seamstress did not let out the dress like I told her? It is still too tight across the bust. I got another letter from Michael's teacher about his behavior, and you know the airline, which I've always hated, has no more first-class seats for our trip to Cancun. My other phone is ringing. Talk to you later."

Jake leaned down and kissed her bald head. "How could anyone love this wicked witch?"

"Jakob let me see you," Ruth said.

Jake knelt and held her hands. She knew from his expression that he could tell she was nauseated from her chemotherapy and radiation treatments.

"Josh says they finally got the right protocol. You look good."

A Developing Country

Ruth did not want to discuss her health. "I know you never wanted to talk about Bessedelya, but I believe you will find what you're looking for."

"*You* tried so hard to find your family. Poland. Israel. All of your searching turned up nothing," Jake reminded her.

"It will be different for you."

"How can you say that? Fifty years later, I don't know how to begin."

"DV, don't vorry," Ruth said. "If you don't discover your history, you may find your future. Maybe you'll find your *Bashert*, the woman you were intended to marry."

An entourage approached the table. Mary Carver, the vice president of the United States was in the middle of the group. Everyone stood.

As Ruth got up she said, "Madame Vice President."

Mrs. Carver said, "Please everyone, sit down. I just came to fuss with my dear friend Ruth. Why do you always turn down my invitations?"

"I tire so easily," Ruth said. "But you know how proud I am of you. I don't have to tell you."

"Yes you do," Mrs. Carver said. "You pushed me so hard. Now I want to hear some compliments even if you don't mean them."

JM approached the table carrying drinks.

"Ruth was my favorite teacher and was about to teach my children when her inconsiderate husband made her stop."

JM put down the drinks and embraced the vice president.

A young man pulled Jake aside. "I'm Mort Plant, the vice president's administrative assistant. You probably know

Mrs. Mitchell is the person most responsible for your being considered by the president."

"I didn't know that," Jake said.

"The senators will be digging for anything to embarrass you at the hearings. Are you prepared for that kind of scrutiny?"

"Some sports writers thought I choked in the Olympics," Jake said.

Plant did not smile. "I don't think the senators will be amused by your sense of humor."

The crowd around them parted and many turned to watch Becky as the celebrity touched Jake on the shoulder. He turned and kissed her cheek.

"Will you be upset if I ask the vice president a few questions?" she asked.

"Don't. Not now," he answered.

"Everyone's buzzing about you. When were you going to tell me you're the favorite to get the big appointment?" she asked.

"Never," Jake said.

"I've got something that will loosen your tongue," she said.

As the vice president and her entourage moved away, Plant turned to Jake and said, "You should be ready to discuss incidents in your life that may surprise your closest friends."

Jake knew that none would be aware of that terrible scene at the hospital, when the doctor came out of the delivery room and told him his first child would be retarded. They could not imagine his wife's screams when he told her they would not be taking their baby home. It would surprise them to know that neither she nor their marriage would recover from that day.

"I'll be prepared," Jake said.

After the gala, Jake and Becky were excited to be alone in their beautiful hotel room. They had not been together for weeks, and it was wonderful to again make love.

Jake wore a towel when he came out of the bathroom. Becky laughed when he stumbled over his clothes strewn over the floor. He picked up his wallet and the group photo of the Africans that had fallen from his pants.

He was looking at the picture when Becky said, "You're so handsome. Look at me, Jake. I'm not getting any younger. You said we would talk about our getting engaged."

Jake looked up. "You're the only one in my life, sweetheart. I've told you that my marriage was too stormy, too painful for me. I need a little more time. After this appointment.."

"In two weeks I fly to Bermuda," she said. "Could we talk then? You'll never guess who I've got an interview with. Are you listening?" Jake nodded. "Can you go with me?"

"I'm going to Bessedelya for a few days."

"Fun City, the big resort in Africa?"

"Not the resort, the capital. I have to check the archives. Get some information."

"You know, honey, you can get a lot of stuff online. And didn't they just report a bombing? It may be dangerous."

"I'll just be there a day or two. Besides, the insurance companies will protect me. Dead, I'll cost them a lot of money."

CHAPTER 10

Before going to the airport, Jake had to show his face at a charity luncheon. A major client's firm was being honored.

When he entered the hotel he gave his luggage to a bellhop and followed him to the front desk. "Please hold these suitcases," he said to the clerk. He pointed to an event described on a bulletin board. The organization would be represented by Rob Copeland, the contemptible son-in-law of the politically powerful owner. "I'll pick them up in a few minutes."

People at the head table were making a presentation, when Jake found several of his friends seated near the back of the room.

"You wouldn't be late if this were a cabinet meeting," said Randy. "And anyway, you should show some respect for the speaker. You are only going to be a secretary, but when the boss dies he will be a president."

"Jake will never be Treasury secretary," Elaine said. "The smart money is on Diego Guzman. His credentials are outstanding, and more important, he was a soccer star at the president's alma mater.

"If you all will be quiet," said Phil, "you may learn something.. They just said Copeland was a naval hero who helped win the last war."

"The schmuck was in special services after Annapolis," Randy clarified. "He told me himself that he scheduled events, booked celebrities and played tennis with the Admirals."

"War is hell," Jack said.

"Where are you going?" asked Randy as Jake headed for the exit. "You just got here."

It was cold and windy when Jake ducked into a taxi and gave the airport destination. He noticed the driver had an African name.

"How long have you been here?" Jake asked.

"Three years," the driver said.

"What are your plans?"

"Get my degree, and then go back to Kenya."

"Have you thought about staying in the states?"

"For sure," the driver said, "but I'm not happy here. Everyone is scared of black men. They look down when they see me. In my country, everyone hugs me."

"Have you heard of Bessedelya?"

"The Switzerland of Africa," the driver said.

"You mean it's a beautiful place?" asked Jake.

"I mean it's a paradise. Nobody wants to leave there, except to study abroad, and then they return."

"So why don't you move to Bessedelya?"

"Too many earthquakes. They scare me to death. If they don't bother you, there's no place like that country. Have you been there?"

"Not since I was a baby."

"What do you do?" the driver asked.

"I tell people what to do, what not to do. Give speeches," he said.

The driver reached back over the seat. "Give me a few of your cards. I'll try to get you some work."

CHAPTER 11

JM and Jake met in Rome when they boarded their plane to Bessedelya. There would be an intermediate stop at Fun City. Seated in first class, they were surrounded by loud, excited sportsmen on their way to the famous resort.

"They say that on any given night, there are more stars in Bessedelya than in heaven," said one gambler.

"In Fun City, in Fun City. Nothing happens in Bessedelya," another man corrected.

When their plane roared down the runway, JM saw Jake grip the armrest and cover his eyes with a mask. JM was reminded of Jake's fear of flying since he'd missed his flight on that September eleventh years ago. Jake had had a seat on the first plane to strike the World Trade Center.

"I want to brief you about my meeting tomorrow," JM said.

Jake was too nervous to care about the next day. "Not now," he said.

JM persisted. "Not even curious to know how the country has grown?"

Jake tried to end the conversation. "We send them money. Every few years there's a coup. A general names himself president for life. He loots the country, and then he is overthrown. America then pledges its support for the new leader."

"Not this country. The people decide every important issue. You get fined if you don't vote."

The laughter and conversations of the gamblers almost drowned out JM's comments. An attractive flight attendant tried to serve drinks and at the same time pull away the hand of a man trying to grope her.

"I don't want to think about Bessedelya. I intend to spend one day, make a few inquiries and go back to the states."

"If I need you to help me at the port meeting, you'll need to know something."

Jake pointed to his watch. "You got one minute."

"They get big income from offshore oil companies and from the Fun City resort and even more from burying nuclear waste. No debt none. They pay cash for all their capital investments. They have high taxes. No involvement with other countries. They say it's none of their business."

Jake was surprised. "I'm sure you advised them to take advantage of the low cost of money, and you were never an isolationist."

"They're just like you. They listen to me, and then do things their way. In any case, they've asked for me to be at this hearing."

"But with Ruth so sick, why make the trip now?"

"She urged me to go. You know Ruth, 'The president and Ali have been our friends. They asked for help, end of story.' She said she'll be fine."

"Okay. What else?" Jake asked. "We only hear about the resort never about Bessedelya. Nobody in the world goes there except you and Ruth."

"They don't permit the big concerts, and they discourage tourists. Even the rich and famous visitors to Fun City aren't welcomed."

"Don't want tourism?" Jake asked.

"It's not that simple. The president doesn't like their values or behavior, and he thinks the huge crowds at events he sees on television could be dangerous.

There was an announcement from the pilot. "We are approaching Fun City. If you are continuing to Bessedelya, please remain on the plane." The announcement was repeated in French.

"Almost since the country was founded, the same man has been reelected president," JM continued. "He lives in a converted army barracks and gets the same pay as the other civil servants. Teachers get the highest pay."

"Fascinating, can I sleep now?" Jake asked. JM nodded.

Jake had covered himself with a blanket and gone to sleep. The raucous passengers exited. Shortly afterward the plane took off for Bessedelya.

JM was reading as Hinda came through the curtains that separated the first-class section from the rest of the plane.

"Joshua Mitchell!" Hinda said.

"Hinda!"

"What brings you...," Hinda started to ask.

"There are hearings on the port project tomorrow," he explained. "The financing is going to be controversial. Ali wanted me to help him defend the plan."

"I've never seen you without Ruth. She's okay?"

"She's waiting for me in Rome. The short trip here would be too rough for her. You know she's going to ask me about the man in your life."

Hinda broke into a smile. "I cut my trip short to see him in the All Star game tomorrow."

"I'm sure the president won't miss that."

Jake groaned.

Hinda lowered her voice. "I hope he doesn't go. He's in a late stage of dementia. Unfortunately, BG's TV stations go out of their way to ridicule him when he gets confused."

Jake was getting angry. "Quiet. Please."

JM pointed to Jake under the blanket. "Our managing partner," he whispered, "has an incurable case of male menopause."

"I can't wait for you to see the clinics. Every town wants a Mitchell Prefab Hospital," she said.

"They were your great idea."

"Your money," Hinda said.

"How's the election going?"

A Developing Country

"It should be an easy win, but Ali is being blamed for a series of terrorist attacks. We don't know who's behind them or what they want."

There was an announcement from the pilot. "We are about to experience some turbulence. Please return to your seats and fasten your seat belts."

"We'll talk later. I have a message for some friends up front," Hinda said. She walked up the aisle and knelt by an old couple.

"Who was that?" Jake asked as he uncovered the blanket from his head.

"One of the most extraordinary women I've ever known, Secretary of education and health, amazing accomplishments."

Half-asleep Jake said, "Tell me about them some other time."

JM was excited. "Who else in the world rid her country of AIDS in the past few years, increased literacy to ninety percent, and she is largely responsible for a new trade zone that links the eastern and southern half of Africa, twenty six countries almost half the continent?"

Hinda came back down the aisle and saw Jake. "The consultant!" she said.

Jake sat up and smiled. "Dr. Malaria?"

JM was startled.

"We're old friends," Jake explained.

"Not so old," Hinda said.

"Where are you sitting?" Jake asked.

Hinda pointed to the back and waved for Jake to join her. He followed but had to stand in the aisle because there were no vacant seats.

"Aren't you the woman who picks up strangers and then takes them to bars?" Jake asked.

"That's me. You here for the port meeting too?"

Jake hesitated. He did not want to explain his search for family history. "Researching African pandemics. Actually I'm looking for the expert I heard at a conference. She really got my attention."

"I'll help you find her." She smiled.

A flight attendant interrupted them and told Jake to return to his seat.

When he told JM about their having met at the Davos Forum, JM said, "She uses her speaking engagements to recruit outstanding people for Bessedelya's colleges and programs. She's always looking for original thinkers and innovators."

As Jake fixed his seat belt, JM said, "Look down there." He pointed to shacks and fences along the beach. "They were known as slave castles. Families were gathered from all over and shipped from right there."

The plane suddenly dipped and then rose. When JM saw his frightened friend grab the armrest, he put his hand on Jake's. "Imagine how our great-grandparents must have suffered. Mine were refugees from Europe, on old ships, suffocating in the heat, freezing in the cold, seasick. The Europeans exploited your people without mercy. For some reason, you and I are survivors. I believe we're here for a purpose."

"Maybe you're right, but I only want to know why I was sold or given away," said Jake.

CHAPTER 12

The Bessedelya airport was busy. As Jake and JM left their plane, they saw two men standing next to a private jet posing for pictures. One of them was short, bald and wearing a dark suit. The tall, handsome man in a safari jacket and a wide-brimmed hat wore a necklace and sunglasses. The logo *BG Industries* was on the tail of the plane.

"The country's biggest private company," said JM. "It's probably a photo op for BG the one in the suit. He's running for president. The guy dressed like a pimp is his brother John."

Outside the terminal, the atmosphere was festive. Musicians played at several locations. There were screams of joy and affection as the incoming passengers entered the building. A huge group had signs welcoming the country's first Nobel laureate.

"Ever seen such a large crowd of students celebrating?" asked Ali.

"Only after sports events," said Jake.

Jake saw a smiling man emerge from the crowd extending his hand to JM. Ali Mohammed was followed by his young daughter Dinna pulling a little dog. The little girl ran past them to hug Hinda, as Ali greeted JM and shook hands with Jake.

"I hope your trip was easy," Ali said. "I'm happy to meet you Mr. Warsaw. Please give me your passports and baggage tickets. I'll walk us through customs."

Jake pointed to the men's room sign and said, "I'll catch up with you."

One wall of the airport was filled with political posters and advertisements. Jake stopped to look at one with Ali standing next to an old man. Because the message on the picture said Ali would continue the great leadership of the past, Jake assumed the man with Ali was the president.

BG's well-crafted posters described his educational achievements and his involvement with many institutions and organizations. He was shown talking with college students saying, "If I'm elected president, Bessedelya will lead Africa into the twenty-first century."

BG and John had noticed Hinda, JM, Ali and Jake together. They saw Ali leave and watched Jake looking at the political posters. BG walked over to Hinda. They kissed, and he welcomed JM. John nodded.

"How does it feel to know you will soon be unemployed?" BG asked Hinda.

"Last I read, Ali was winning. Your television station and papers are saying the same thing," she replied.

"Not to worry. You haven't seen the new polls. I've got the momentum now," BG said.

"And they want BG to close down your abortion clinics and stop your porno shows on TV," John added. "The people are really concerned with Ali's Islamic brothers."

A Developing Country

As Jake came toward them, BG asked, "Who's the black American?"

Before JM could answer, Hinda said, "I thought you might have recognized Jake Warsaw one of America's top political consultants. He's here to make sure Ali is our next president." Then, hiding her smile, she added, "Buy me lunch next week?"

"Yeah, sure. I'll call you," BG said as he signaled the BG employees carrying his luggage to follow. He watched Hinda and JM laughing as they walked away.

"Well what do you know?" asked John. "Ali's hired a big advisor."

"She's bullshitting. I know Hinda. And Ali doesn't think he needs an advisor."

"Mother said not to take any chances." John used his cell phone to take pictures of Jake. "So I'm not taking any chances."

He called over one of the BG employees and pointed out Jake and JM.

"John, don't do anything stupid," BG said as he walked away.

John knew his dirty tricks were unappreciated by his brother. *My hired men are playing rough,* he thought, *but it's necessary. BG doesn't understand elections. It's pass or fail. We're definitely bringing attention to Ali's religion. Polls show it. The bombers will be killed as soon as they're caught. When BG's elected, I'll conduct an inquiry. No one will connect me. If BG finds out, he'll be furious, but he'll get over it. When he becomes president, he'll thank God, our parents, his teachers, his children, everybody but me. One day they'll get it. They'll realize that the smarter I work, the more successful he gets.*

Ali returned, said good-bye to Hinda, took his little girl's hand and started toward the exit.

Hinda gave Jake one of her cards. "If you have some time, let's get together."

"I'd like that."

Ali said to JM and Jake, "Let's go this way. My driver's got your bags. We'll take a back road to town. Try to avoid all the traffic."

CHAPTER 13

A mile away from the airport, a BG company van almost passed and then swerved in front of them, forcing Ali's driver to brake and turning their car in a circle.

Ali grabbed his daughter Dinna. "That crazy bastard, you all right?" he asked her.

JM's cell phone rang. "It's Sam Goldman," he said to Jake. "You know, the PR guy." JM was trying to use his little phone. "I can't hear you Sam."

Ali said, "Give it to Dinna."

Dinna took the cell phone and turned on the speaker.

"Jake's interviews in the *Times* and the *Post* were not good," Sam said. "And his article in the *Journal* criticizing the bankers' bonuses and their terrible mortgages could have been more balanced. Some rumor about him having a serious environmental problem."

JM was tired. "Sammy, Sammy, put out the story that he came from a dysfunctional family, lived on food stamps."

"Get serious," Sam said. "Jake's become a long shot. He'll need some strong references. Are there any people there who can help him?"

"He's got relatives here who are cannibals," JM said. "I'm sure we can get their endorsement. They came back to Africa when they realized they weren't vicious enough to survive on Wall Street."

It had started to rain again. The driver pointed to a line of trucks stopped at a border crossing. Several men were trying to move something in the road.

When Ali told him to bypass the traffic jam by driving through the tent city on the right, Jake asked," Why such a development here?"

"Immigrants are investigated, kept here sometimes for a few days. Some need months of orientation".

"Are they worth the trouble?" Jake asked.

"They bring an energy and determination you can only get from a survivor. They don't know anything that can't be done."

A border policeman stopped them, and the driver rolled down his window. "We got a rough bunch of new arrivals," he warned. "They don't want to turn in their weapons. We are looking for a few who tried to get away."

He waved them on. After driving a few hundred yards, they heard gunshots and saw people running. Suddenly there was a thump on the car. A face and hand were mashed up against the window. Dinna screamed.

Ali told the driver to stop. He opened the door and got out. When a rock hit the car, he jumped back inside and ordered the driver, "Keep going! Don't stop!" They drove in tense silence for a few miles.

"The president has always helped immigrants," Ali said. "We spend weeks explaining to them the laws and the punishments if they break our rules. We give them their own land and shelter even loans. Getting them settled should be easier."

"Getting to the hotel should be easier," JM said.

The rain stopped as they approached and crossed a beautiful modern bridge. A signpost showed directions and distances to the downtown of the capital and to several other cities.

Jake was suddenly apprehensive. What awaited him on the other side of this river? Would he find any family members alive? What would they remember about his parents? Would their reputations affect his presidential appointment?

Below the bridge, Jake saw an old man and woman come out from under the trees walking to the river. They were carrying fishing rods. It reminded him of a wonderful trip to Wyoming and momentarily allowed him to forget the impending meeting with people who might change his life.

CHAPTER 14

The hotel was an unpretentious four-story building in the center of the city. A train station and parking lot were across from the hotel. When they arrived from the airport, the street was congested with traffic and pedestrians.

As a bellhop took their luggage inside, Ali told JM, "The hearings start at ten thirty. I'll pick you up at nine thirty. Is that too early, Mr. Mitchell?"

JM shook his head.

"Mr. Warsaw," Ali continued, "all family records are kept over there in that government building. When you finish your search, call me if you want to join us. We'll be at the hotel." Ali gave Jake his business card. "I'd be happy to take you out tonight, but I assume you may want to rest from your trip."

"I am tired," JM said. "Go home to your family. We'll be okay."

Ali pointed up the street. "If you get hungry, there's a very nice bar that serves good food just up the next corner."

"What do you know about bars?" JM asked. "And when did you start drinking whisky?"

"Who said I drink? I go for the music and the buffet," Ali said. "I'll see you in the morning."

Jake's room was spacious. The bellhop opened the balcony doors, pulled back the bedspread and removed a large black bug.

"They're harmless," he said as he threw it out. "We were told that they were brought here from Florida."

He then went into the bathroom and turned on the water in the shower and sink. The water was brown before it turned clear. A housekeeper knocked and then entered rolling in a cart with a bowl of fruit, flowers and bottled water.

"Our water is safe to drink. You don't need bottled," she said.

Jake went on the balcony and saw a line of people. "What are they waiting for? There, by that two-story wooden building."

"To see the president," she said, "until seven o'clock unless he is too tired or unless there are boxing matches on the TV."

Jake was astounded. *I can't remember when our presidents had regular face to face contact with common people. But is it really necessary? Lobbyists explain each piece of legislation, and polls tell him what the people are thinking. Our country's too big for personal handshakes. He gets everything. It's just filtered.*

Jake held out five dollar bills for the bellhop and housekeeper. Neither accepted the gratuity.

CHAPTER 15

J](**ake was not ready to** sleep. He changed clothes, rode the elevator down and walked outside. Families, couples and children were in the streets now free of cars. Jake stopped to listen to some musicians and watch the many roller skaters in the train station parking lot. After a short walk, he found the bar Ali had recommended.

A singer with a multicolored hat sang reggae music. Jake saw a long table filled with smiling young people surrounding an old lady. She laughed as they did a "wave" when she got up to go to the buffet table.

Jake went to inspect the large assortment of food but did not notice the lady filling her plate. When he brushed up against her, she looked at him and dropped her food.

"Eedel!" she gasped.

"I'm sorry. *Je regret*," Jake said as a waiter rushed over to clean up the mess.

"Eedel!" the old lady repeated.

"I don't understand. *Je ne comprehend pas. Je suis American,*" Jake said.

The woman, too embarrassed to face Jake, walked back to her table.

Jake started to follow her but decided instead to get a drink at the bar.

A well-dressed man standing there laughed. "All of us darkies look alike. But hey brother, it's okay. We all come from the same street."

Back in his hotel room, Jake showered and looked in the mirror. He thought of the words of the man at the bar. "All alike, and come from the same street." He knew he was nothing like his African cousins.

Jake stretched out on the bed and started to daydream. It was the fifties. He held his mother's hand as they walked out of the country club's kitchen. All the white men had stood and applauded when they gave her the Foster Mother of the Year award. He remembered thanking the men he caddied for when they got him a scholarship to the exclusive Boston Latin School and the powerful people he met during the summers he worked on the Cape.

He was at college with his blonde girlfriend after the Princeton graduation. His Ivy Club brothers handed him a sign that said, Make Love, Not War, as he got into her convertible. He recalled the publicity when he became the first black editor of the *Review* at law school and the calls after the news programs showed him testifying before Congressional committees or meeting with world leaders. He was not from the same street as the brothers.

CHAPTER 16

John's BMW sedan pulled up to the hotel entrance. A pretty woman got out and opened the back door. She took out a gym bag and grabbed the handle of a flat, square box. When she leaned inside, John gave her a picture of Jake, a vial of clear liquid and cash.

"You said you want this man to be real sore. If you want to hurt him, you'd better get somebody else," the masseuse said. "I'm a professional."

"You got me wrong," John said. "This guy told me he didn't want a regular massage like you give an old woman. He likes it rough." He pointed to the little bottle. "This here is like Viagra."

She hesitated. "Look Mr. Gee, I don't want to give somebody stuff without telling them, and I sure as hell ain't going to hurt anybody."

John said, "You know me, and I'm telling you, if it don't feel right, or if he's not happy with your work, you can leave."

She counted the money, closed the car door and smiled at the doorman as she walked into the hotel.

A Developing Country

Jake was in his room on his laptop when the phone rang. He put down his glass of water. The front desk wanted to know if everything was satisfactory.

"Everything is good. Wait," Jake said. "I don't have a bar in the room. Could you send up a bottle of tequila and some ice? Take your time."

There was a knock at the door. A pretty woman with a gym bag and a folded table stood there.

"I am a massage therapist. I was sent to help you relax after such a long trip."

He glanced at her gym bag. "Come in. What did you bring?"

She entered the room, put down the table, and took some jars and small packages from the bag. "These are massage oils. These are cigarettes that will make you relax. These are condoms," she said. "And these papers are from the State Health Department that tells when I was checked. Can I be of service?"

"Sure," Jake said.

She began to set up the massage table and turned on the TV with the remote. "You and I have to fill out this form," she said. "I'm required to watch classes on TV about black history and AIDS and other stuff. We get tested on it and can't work if we don't pass. I can turn the sound off because I know the condom lesson pretty good." She turned down the sound.

On the television, a frightened woman was surrounded by several men. As she was held by one of them and approached by another, the scene was abruptly cut. The story continued, but the pretty girl changed channels. She stopped briefly on another program that had a man performing oral sex on a woman and then changed that channel.

The masseuse explained, "The censors are strict. Hurting people is not allowed to be shown, giving pleasure is okay."

"What if a citizen wants to watch the violence?" Jake asked as he climbed on to the massage table.

"You can buy DVDs or see the stuff on your computer."

She continued to change the channels. She stopped when she came to a classroom demonstration. The teacher was placing a condom on a dummy's penis. The camera moved to a tattoo below the belly button. A printed message on the screen explained that any HIV-positive person must be registered with the Health Department and have such a mark in that place.

The masseuse changed the channel until she came to Hinda speaking and then turned up the sound. A woman was singing in the background. "This teacher gives us our health certificates or else we can't work. She's mean as a snake." She laughed. "She says if we don't learn about our history, if we don't protect ourselves, if we don't stop whining about how bad we got it, she'll send us back where we came from. But we love her to pieces."

Jake was surprised to see Hinda on a simple set with portraits of famous black people in the background. She stood between pictures of Bessie Smith and Langston Hughes.

"Ninety years ago, most people had little money," Hinda said. "But even in the terrible Depression when few had jobs, more than eight million Bessie Smith records were sold. She brought the new sounds of blues and jazz. Then she was in a car accident. Because of her skin color, the hospitals would not take her in. When she was finally able to be treated, it was too late. Bessie Smith was dead. Whenever you want to feel the heart and soul of that period, listen to her wonderful voice."

Jake went to the bathroom and closed the door. The masseuse poured the vial of liquid into Jake's half-filled water glass. When Jake returned to the table, she applied some ointment and began to rub his body.

Hinda now stood next to a picture of Langston Hughes. She read, "So we stand here on the edge of hell, in Harlem/ and look out on the world and wonder/ what we gonna do/ in the face of what we remember."

"I remember," said the masseuse. "I was a slave a nobody until I came here. What we gonna do? We gonna be a somebody."

She kneaded Jake's shoulders and then gently held his head in her hands.

Jake was fixated on her breasts.

"I feel a lot of tension," said the woman. Suddenly she jerked his head.

"Jesus Christ," Jake grunted.

She then reached her arms under his arms.

When she yanked his shoulders together, he felt his skeleton crack and screamed, "Wait a goddamn minute!"

"You're okay. I'm a professional," she said as she pushed her knuckles and elbows into his back.

Jake groaned and rolled off the table. He eased himself to his knees, struggled to stand up and spilled the glass of water.

They heard a knock on the door and "Room service."

The masseuse was frightened. Her client was in pain. If she had hurt him, she'd be out of the program. Why had she put something in his drink? How could she have trusted that crazy Mr. Gee? She grabbed her box of ointments and papers, threw them in her gym bag, folded the table and went to the door. She calmly walked past the startled bellhop as Jake, in great agony, fell on the bed.

CHAPTER 17

In the morning Jake hobbled to the lobby. The bellhop told him the shortest way to the government building, and he went out into the busy street. Men in sport coats walked next to lines of schoolchildren in uniforms following their teachers. Nuns, Sikh and veiled women mingled with street vendors.

Jake noticed there were keys in many of the parked cars. A convertible with its top down had packages on the seats. He remembered JM telling him that you could leave things anywhere, and nobody would disturb them.

Jake bought a sweet roll and cup of coffee and then proceeded toward the government building. He came to a speakers' corner where there were ten rows of benches and two sixty-inch television monitors. A shed roof covered two unattended microphones and a TV camera. A sign read that there would be a "port hearing" between ten thirty and twelve thirty. Jake's back hurt. He sat down, finished his coffee and continued to the government building.

BG and John were a block from the government building when they saw Jake limping toward the election offices that they had just left. Neither saw Jake walk past that office and into the room marked Records/Archives.

"Still think Hinda was joking?" John asked. BG was speechless. "Don't worry. I'll think of something."

A woman with grey hair was sitting at a long table working on two ledgers in the archives offices when Jake arrived. Books were spread out before her, and the table had two computer terminals.

"I'm trying to learn about a family that used to live here," Jake said. "I'm from America."

She looked up and smiled. "Come sit near me. We have almost everyone's genealogy."

Jake walked around the counter and joined her. She shut her ledgers and set them to the side.

"These people were here fifty years ago," he told her.

Her smile faded. "I may have spoken too quickly. We began storing records about forty years ago. We have few records from before that period."

"I don't understand." He felt crestfallen. Had he traveled all this way for nothing?

"Information from those years was not recorded by government order."

"Why not?" Jake asked, incredulous.

A Developing Country

"The Founders believed the only hope for reconciliation was to lose the reminders of those bloody times," she said. "More strict laws, hearings, exposure of the guilty parties, nothing stopped the aggression. They thought that if there were few records, no monuments, no pictures showing victors or victims, eventually people might forget why they hated each other."

"Obviously, they were naïve. How can people become more civilized unless they learn from their history?"

She raised her eyebrows at his response. "It depends on what you've learned. Did you Americans become more humane when you invented better ways to kill? You found reasons to burn heretics, massacre Indian nations, lynch colored people and drop atomic bombs. You learned how to destroy from great distances with aircraft carriers and now smart bombs and drones. With all you've learned, are you more civilized?"

Jake replied, "I'd like to think we are making progress."

"Have you been here long?"

"Only a few hours," he said.

"Visit our different towns. You'll see ancient enemies living near each other. Hutus next to Watutsis, Palestinians next to Israelis, Pakistanis near Indians."

"I've no time. Can you suggest any other sources?" he asked.

"I'm sure there are elders who can help you. Before you leave, you see that man over there? He'll take your DNA sample. Maybe we'll find a match."

CHAPTER 18

People had begun to gather at the speakers' corner as Jake walked back to the hotel. He found JM and Ali finishing breakfast and discussing the port project. The three men walked outside where the driver was waiting to take them to Congress. The hearing would begin in less than an hour.

Shortly after they left, a hitchhiker in an army uniform with a rifle appeared on the road. The driver asked Ali if he should pick him up. Ali nodded. The soldier was a girl.

"Aren't you somebody?" she asked Ali.

"Ali Mohammed, the vice president."

"Too much of our taxes go to immigrants," she said without a preamble. "They get better homes. We have to serve in the army one month every year. They have computers and cars. For all we help them, they don't do shit."

"Does your family have enough food and water? Do you have jobs?" Ali asked.

A Developing Country

"Here, yes, but in my homeland, my people fight for their lives. Why don't you send our army, guns, something to help them?"

"We don't interfere in civil wars, and we're not the neighborhood's policeman," Ali said.

"But it's genocide. You must do something."

"We can't solve every country's problems."

"You don't solve Bessedelya's problems. You ignore the women in my town. They must wear certain clothes, can't go to college or play sports. Their parents choose the husbands."

"Your family came here to escape problems in their homeland. They found a safe haven where they can follow their customs with few exceptions. We will interfere if we believe your punishments are inhumane. If your women wish to leave your community, they would be welcome everywhere in our country."

"You old guys just don't get it. You should move out of the way and let younger people run things. They'd know what we want. Driver I get off here."

He pulled to the side of the road. She took her backpack, climbed out of the car and slammed the door.

"When I count my voters, I'll put her down as undecided," Ali said.

"Will BG get her vote?" Jake asked.

"Not if she really knew him," Ali explained. "He is very smart, but privately he likes to say he is not a people person. I don't think he's empathetic. Look at the president. Not an educated man. Everybody tells me about a policy of his that they hate. Like the soldier girl. People on television always make fun of him. But he's always reelected. Why? Why do they vote for him? I think the people know he acts from his heart."

Up ahead, huge plastic-covered greenhouses appeared. The driver pointed out an old car in the parking area that was missing a hubcap. "Isn't that the president's car?"

"Speak of the devil," Ali said. "Pull over. I'll just be a minute."

Ali walked toward a group of people watching a demonstration of drip irrigation. The president and a few others were lying in the dirt. When the president saw Ali, he got up and they walked a few yards away.

Ali gestured and seemed to yell at the old man. When the president slammed his hat to the ground, Ali stormed back to the car.

Jake could not resist. "It looked like the president disagreed with you."

"The place he wants to settle these immigrants has bad water," Ali said. "The Israelis convinced him they have a system where magnetically charged pipes will take out the heavy minerals. The old son of a bitch can hardly read, but he's always experimenting."

"What would BG do?" Jake asked.

"He wouldn't let all of these people in the country. He wants investors and big corporations and scientists. He says we should admit educated people who will create jobs."

CHAPTER 19

The port hearing was held in a converted airplane hangar that now housed the Congress. The parking lot was filled. Ali, JM, and Jake were following a crowd walking toward the entrance when a man approached Ali.

"I'm Fred Glazer with the United Press. Have you time for a few questions?"

"Sorry, Mr. Glazer," Ali said, "see me later. I'm needed inside now."

"Jake," JM said as he and Ali continued to the building. "Maybe you could help him?"

From his expression, it was clear Jake was not enthusiastic about his assignment.

"Are you here as an expert on this project?" the journalist asked and gave Jake his business card.

"I am."

"Have you talked to the people who'll be affected by the Port?"

Jake shook his head.

"Have you seen the place where they want to build?"

"No," Jake said.

"Is the rumor true that the US military is behind this development?"

"It could be. They haven't discussed it with me."

"And you're here to advise the voters?"

"You don't seem to understand, Fred. Once we experts are hired, we usually don't want to be confused with the facts."

An entourage walked behind Jake and entered the building.

The journalist said, "We can continue this informative interview later. Hinda Raisal just went in. She's usually good at stirring things up."

The building was almost full. Jake and Glazer found seats near Ali and JM. A model of the proposed port was on a table. Television cameras crept along the ceiling and projected the model on two large screens. BG and John were seated in the back.

BG was speaking. "..and we cannot afford not to begin this project now."

The crowd's cheering stopped when Ali stood.

"Why is BG so eager to put us in debt? Is his tourist business in trouble? Does his bank need business? Remember our president's words of wisdom, 'Lenders are like slave ships with shoes.'"

Many in the audience applauded.

The chairwoman of the hearing, Martha Jamerson, saw that Hinda had taken a seat near the entrance. She said, "Welcome, Dr. Raisal. You were missed at previous meetings."

"Thank you, Madame Chairman," Hinda said. "I've watched some of the proceedings on television."

"We'd be interested in your comments, Dr. Raisal."

"The proposed port will create many good jobs, and the revenue from the operations will help reduce our taxes. Your advisors have done an excellent job answering most of the questions. You are to be commended."

"You said 'answered *most* of the questions.'"

"I did not hear them address any environmental issues. Perhaps they were covered in the transcripts," Hinda said.

"What are your concerns?" the leader asked.

"What will happen to the large wildlife refuge and the wetlands next to the area where they would build or the seabed there? Will any of the construction disturb our largest aquifer of fresh water? As you know, it would be ruined if it's mixed with saltwater," Hinda said.

"I thought I understood that you are in favor of the port," the chairwoman said.

"I think we should build a port like the model," Hinda said, "but I believe it should be built somewhere that does not harm the environment."

When translators repeated Hinda's comments, the audience burst into shouts and arguments.

John stood up and was recognized. "Does Dr. Raisal think saving five hundred wild animals is as important as creating five hundred new jobs? Please explain to her that we need the new port to pay for her goddamned whorehouses?"

A woman in the audience stood and waved her hand. "Those whorehouses have stopped our AIDS epidemic."

When several people started pushing and shoving, the journalist gestured for Jake to follow him. "Welcome to our democracy," he said.

As they walked outside, Jake said to the journalist, "An ambitious plan. Are you for it?"

He nodded. "Very much so. Imagine the imports and exports that will pass through Bessedelya. As other countries connect to us with railroads and highways, the economy of the entire continent will explode."

"You are talking about an enormous investment," Jake said. "It will require strong public support, but the people seem to be happy with what they have."

"They should be," Glazer said. "We've lived a charmed life, but this is the twenty-first century. Change is inevitable, and we'll need leaders to persuade the people that the opportunities are worth the sacrifices."

"Can Ali do the job?"

"I'm not sure. He has the qualities to be a good leader, but I'm afraid that as long as the president lives, he'd be too loyal to him to institute the needed policy changes."

"What about BG?"

"Can he be a good leader if he lacks a passion for the job? Most think the only reason he's running is because of his mother. She'll do whatever she can to see that he gets elected."

"Is she any different than everyone everywhere who wants the power and prestige of that office?" Jake asked.

"Actually we have a person who doesn't want the position or the power but would be a great leader. The people love her because they know she fights for them, and I think they are excited by her vision of a united Africa. You just heard her speak."

CHAPTER 20

As soon as they were away from the congress building, Jake dialed his office and hit the speaker button on his cell phone.

"We've been trying to reach Mr. Mitchell," Kay said. "Ruth had a serious reaction to her chemo. We have no information on her condition, but we were able to get her on a plane home from Italy. I'll call as soon as I hear something. Some scary news, your doctor's office got the results of your procedure. He wants to see you as soon as you return."

Jake said to Glazer, who had overheard the call, "Fred please tell the man with Ali, Mr. Mitchell, to come here right away. I'm going to check on the next plane to the states."

Jake was on hold when JM came out, followed by Hinda and the journalist. "JM, Ruth's not well. She's on her way to Washington. The best connection is a plane that leaves in about half an hour. We've got to run."

JM collapsed on a nearby bench.

Hinda had used her phone to make a call and was talking when Ali came from the building. She said, "Ali, take JM to the hotel to get his things and then to the airport."

"We'll miss the flight," Jake said.

"I just talked to flight control. If Ali's with him, they'll hold the plane until JM gets there. They only have one seat. You'll have to catch the next plane," she said.

"Jake," JM said as he got in the car with Ali and his driver, "Don't rush back. You've still got work to do." They drove away.

Hinda said to Jake, "I'm going to the port. Do you want to see what JM's been working on?"

Jake said, "Yes I would."

"Well wait here. I'll be back in a few minutes." Hinda went to the lady's room to fix her makeup and hair.

Many people were beginning to leave the hearing. Three old men walked past Jake and Glazer. One did a double take and then pulled his friends back to stare at Jake.

He said, "Eedel?"

Jake was curious. "Were you talking about me?"

The old men laughed. "We thought you were somebody."

Hinda returned and said to Glazer, "Fred, the president is having a welcoming party tonight for some new settlers. I'm sorry it's the last minute, but I'm inviting you and Mary. I don't know if she's told you, but I've been one of her patients for about six months."

"I'll be damned. She never discusses her patients, but she does love you. What time should we be there?"

"Try to be there about six thirty."

CHAPTER 21

Before Jake could sit in Hinda's car, she had to move laundry and medical supplies. Several people who wanted to simply thank her for various deeds, interrupted her car cleaning. As they drove from the parking lot, a bright colored BMW caught Jake's eye. A few minutes later, he noticed that same car following them. John was driving.

"Should you be afraid of BG and John?" Jake asked.

"We grew up together," Hinda said. "BG and I studied in the states at the same time at different schools. He was always there for me whether I needed him or not, like a big brother. John's the unsuccessful oldest boy. He dropped out of college and was kicked out of the border patrol. I think it's been hard for him always being compared to his little brother.

"Listen," she said, "I've got one important stop. Do you like sports?" Jake nodded. "We are going to catch a few innings of a baseball game."

Traffic came to a stand still. A cart full of produce had turned on its side. Two cars had collided trying to avoid the spill. A police car was on the scene. There was going to be a long delay.

Hinda pulled down a side street and parked. She took a pair of tennis shoes from a gym bag in the back, leaned against the car and put them on.

"You see that stadium behind those buildings?" she asked. "It's about a mile from here. I've got to run. You want to wait here, or do you think you could meet me there? If you walk, you will be there in twenty minutes."

"I'll go with you." He put his sport coat on the seat and rolled up his cuffs.

Hinda walked through an opening in the guardrail and started to jog. Jake tried to hurdle the rail, slipped on some loose pebbles, and fell on his face. Hinda ran back to help the embarrassed American athlete.

"Are you all right?"

Jake was mortified. "Yeah, go on. I'll find you."

Jake brushed himself off and began to jog. He saw a shortcut through the big cemetery in front of the stadium and began running until he saw a bench, where he sat and rested. He took off his shoe to remove a few pebbles and wiped his head with a handkerchief.

He looked up and saw a woman watching him. Her face was strangely familiar. She wore a dashiki. He noticed she had been having a picnic with a man and two small girls in the shade of some trees. When she offered a ladle of water, he accepted the drink without hesitation, thanked her and continued his run.

CHAPTER 22

It was the last inning of a Little League All Star game, and most of the crowd was standing. Jake worked his way to the empty seat Hinda had saved beside her. She and her friends cheered as two runners crossed the plate. They screamed at the umpire as the third runner was thrown out.

Hinda did not see Jake intercept cups and debris thrown at her, but she heard the father of one player say, "What a throw. My boy doesn't know the meaning of the word *quit*."

Hinda replied, "He doesn't know his ass from third base," but the noise drowned out her response as the pitcher faced the batter who could tie the game.

The boy in the batter's box looked around the stands until he saw Hinda and broke into a big grin. She waved, and he touched the brim of his cap. When the batter struck out to end the game, Hinda turned to Jake with tears in her eyes and buried her head in his chest. She wiped her face and then hurried to the field to hug her son and his teammates.

A Developing Country

Driving from the ballgame to the Port, Hinda pointed out a fish farm and a plant that was producing energy from algae. When they approached a huge nuclear power plant, she said, "More than half our electricity comes from atomic energy and windmills."

"Never, after any of my matches, did anyone from my family hug me," Jake said. "I was born here. I was hoping to find some family or people who knew them."

"Did you check our archives offices?" she asked.

"They couldn't help me. Said there were elderly people who might. I'm sure your husband would have been proud of your son today."

"When we were at medical school, and he was far from his family and friends, he could deal with my being too black. He let everyone know he was a fourth-generation American. When I told him I was pregnant, he wouldn't see me anymore. Marriage was out of the question. Proud of an African son?" She shook her head.

"Ashamed is bad, but could you imagine parents giving away their son?"

Hinda saw the torment in Jake's demeanor. "Rape has become a weapon of war," she began. "When a wife was made pregnant by force, by a stranger, many men had to make a painful decision. Must I continue to work to feed the child of another man? Can I even live with a woman who mothered that child? Jake, you cannot begin to imagine your parents' agony with that decision."

"Maybe there was no rape," Jake said.

"And maybe they saved your life. You could never have had the success you've enjoyed if you had grown up here."

"So I should thank them for giving me away?"

"Just don't judge them," she said.

CHAPTER 23

Hinda and Jake drove by billboards that advertised safari tours, electric cars and marinas. One billboard showed bare-breasted women enjoying the beach at a fancy hotel.

As they approached the industrial area of the port, they came to a stoplight. A pickup truck with a BG logo pulled up alongside them. Several burly white men sat in the open bed of the truck, and two were in the cab. One of them waved to Hinda.

"Goddamn yahoos," she said. "They work on the oil rigs. They should make them stay there. Shouldn't be allowed to mix with our people."

"The whiteness may rub off?" Jake laughed. "Probably nice guys if you got to know them."

A Developing Country

The BG employees were on their way to a large boat-storage building. Inside, expensive speedboats and small yachts were stacked three high. About thirty men in BG uniforms stood listening to John as he handed out pictures of Jake.

"You get a thousand dollars if you find this man by himself and can get him into your truck," John said. "Beat the shit out of him, but don't kill him. I want him to be able to take the next plane out of here. If you get caught, I don't know you."

CHAPTER 24

At a fork in the road, a billboard described the amusements at beaches a few miles to the left. Hinda turned right. As they approached the waterfront, a huge container ship was moving out of sight behind the buildings.

Jake was surprised to see the variety of vessels and so much activity. Watching men on a floating derrick positioning a bulldozer onto a barge, he thought of our high tech world, and how little had changed in the design of great lifting cranes, and that the stevedores' jobs too were the same as they were more than a thousand years ago.

Hinda pulled into a parking space next to a building where men were moving boxes into a refrigerated truck. A sign read Raisal Seafood Company.

"It looks like you'll meet my family," she said.

All the men stopped working when they saw Hinda and Jake get out of the car. Just then another man came out of the building accompanied by a young woman and man in border patrol uniforms.

"Jakob Warsaw, say hello to my stepbrothers Luke and Mayer. This fat man is Reuben and the beautiful lady is Sara, his daughter. I don't know the officer."

"I'm Captain Manno. Pleased to meet you. Your niece speaks of you often."

Reuben said, "They told me the terrorist activity is unusual."

The captain appeared hesitant to discuss this information until Sara said, "Hinda was a top intel officer. I'm sure her friend is okay. Tell them what happened."

"They were spotted by our drones last night," Manno said. "We alerted the big Moslem town south of Lake Sadat and flew in our soldiers. When we confronted them, there was a brief firefight. They carried no identification. One survived. I'm told he is talking."

"The border patrols keep our country secure, Jake. I sleep well knowing little Sara is on the job," Mayer teased.

"We must go," Manno said to Sara, and they walked to their car.

"I've got to go too," Hinda said. "Do you have some fish for me?"

Luke called over one of his men and told him what to bring.

"I want to talk to the man who could keep you away today," Mayer said to Hinda.

"I had to be at the port hearing," she said.

"Bullshit. You could have used any of the speakers' corners," Mayer said.

"And she's wearing makeup," Luke said.

Hinda laughed, "Some clams or langoustines, if you have some."

"You think one box is enough?" Reuben asked.

"Maybe another box," Hinda said.

A man on a forklift had brought boxes of fish and began loading the back of Hinda's SUV.

"Papa has a party tonight," Luke explained to Jake.

"You're going, aren't you, Jake?" Hinda asked.

"I don't know what JM has planned," Jake said.

"He was going. I'm sure. You'll get to meet the president," Hinda said. "Jake and JM came to help you guys with the port project. The least you could do is show him around and buy him lunch." She got into her car. "Tell your taxi. Six, six thirty will be good."

Reuben waved to Hinda and turned to his brothers. "Mayer, you're the only one who doesn't smell. Why don't you take Jake to Tanta Ruby's?"

As they drove along the waterfront road, both men were attracted by the massive oil platforms far out to sea. ""Impressive aren't they? They give us a lot of business." A marina appeared with many beautiful boats. Most were side by side. Some were tied to clusters of pilings away from shore. "A lot of real rich people stop here on the way to Fun City." He pointed to a beach a few miles up the coast. "That's where they want to build the port."

They pulled into a large parking lot next to a sprawling old building.

"This place has great food," Mayer said.

"It doesn't look like a restaurant," Jake said.

"It's the best and the only rest home for thirty miles."

Tanta Ruby's was a state licensed and carefully controlled brothel. One section of the building was a restaurant.

A large sign at the entrance read State Health Department requirements- Everyone must have an identification card. Everyone must be tested before getting service. All questions on the admission form must be fully answered.

A doctor and two nurses worked with the applicants. Sex workers wore plain uniforms with name tags.

Mayer and Jake walked by the brothel's waiting room. They saw well-dressed men and women between the ages of fifteen and sixty-five. Some were watching television. Some played videogames.

They went into the restaurant and sat by a piano. Mayer waved at a man being seated in the corner. It was BG's brother John.

Jake was astonished at the apparent general acceptance of the brothel concept. "If we could get the franchise for this operation in the fifty states, we'd make a fortune."

"Few cities have one," Mayer said. "The residents decide if they want them or not."

"What made you decide to put one here?"

"It wasn't easy. The religious leaders went wild, held big rallies. But Hinda wouldn't back down. She'd say, 'We can't cure the disease, so we must have a prevention plan or we'll all die.'"

"How'd you vote?"

"I voted against. We were embarrassed by her whole idea. At first it was a big joke, a whorehouse called a rest home. Now they're taken for granted like post offices."

Two teenaged girls were on their way out of the brothel. When they saw Mayer, they came to the table. "Mr. Raisal, Mary was so good in the school play."

"Thanks girls. You like this restaurant?" he asked.

"I've never eaten here," one said. "too expensive. We like the men at this rest home." When another teenager called them from the door of the dining room, they said good-bye and left.

"My daughter's friends," Mayer said. "Hinda insisted we wouldn't succeed unless everybody, and she meant *everybody*, had access to a safe experience."

"I saw a brochure at the front desk. If I read it right, the services aren't cheap. Suppose you can't afford it?"

"Poor people get something like your food stamps. Parents pay for their kids. Hinda explained that AIDS was not just killing careless people. She showed that we were losing our best people, people with special skills, rich and poor. I think we realized we had no other choice. We had to find a way to protect everybody."

"Like food stamps. Your sister's a genius," Jake said. He looked at the nearby piano. "Do you think they'd mind?"

When Mayer shook his head, Jake went over and sat on the stool. "Playing piano in a cathouse," he laughed. "I can die now. What was that about your sister being away today?"

"Oh. This was her day to go with us on the boat. Almost never misses," he said.

"What does she do on the boat?"

"She helps everybody. Actually makes a big difference."

"I think she made a difference at the Congress today."

"Not too much, I hope. We know she can change people's minds."

"She wanted the port at a different location, and she raised some environmental issues. But- John approached their table- Jake continued, "I still think we've got the votes."

John reached out to shake Mayer's hand and asked, "Got the votes?"

"You heard an expert, John." Mayer laughed. "And you know an expert usually is 'a man from out of town.' Well, Jake's from out of town, so he should know."

CHAPTER 25

Makeeba was **unloading the boxes** of fish from Hinda's car. She had walked into the president's house and stopped to talk to a housekeeper who was mopping the floor.

"How's your mother today Rachel?"

"She had a good night. Thank you for asking," Rachel said. "I'm worried about the president. He was watching the port business on the TV. The announcer said the white man next to Ali was an advisor. When the camera showed the black man next to the white man, the president made some noise and started to cry. He said 'eagle' or something like that. Then he went outside. He's in the back now."

Hinda walked to the tables in the backyard, where helpers were cleaning and preparing vegetables. The president was admiring the seafood. She knew there was only one eagle in Papa's mind.

Hinda kissed him on the cheek. "Expecting a big crowd tonight?"

A Developing Country

President Simba was happy to see Hinda. "Not so many, some Ethiopian children from Israel and a group from India. I heard that JM had to go home, any word about his wife?"

"No."

"I don't want his friend here," he said.

"We can't uninvite him."

"Think of an excuse. Tell him I'm sick."

"I'll keep him away from you. What does this have to do with 'Eedel'?"

The president just looked at her and shook his head.

CHAPTER 26

John **drove to his family's** yacht. BG was standing at a railing near his parents reading a magazine.

"All this bombing. What the hell's happening John?" William Gee asked.

"They're fanatics, Ali's cousins. Where they come from, life has no value."

"But here they can live anyway they want. We leave everyone alone. The president told me we should put up a Statue of Liberty like the one in New York. He loves those words, 'Give me your tired people, the wretched people who want to be free.'"

John had a different translation. "It's another way of saying, 'Give me your garbage.' These people will ruin the country, and if BG doesn't win, the problem will get worse."

"Doesn't win?" BG's mother asked.

"Ali's brought in a big political consultant," John said. "I just came from Tanta Ruby's, and I heard him say they have the votes to win the election."

BG's mother was alarmed. "How's he know they have the votes? Who is this man?"

"I'll know more about him soon. My men will get him."

"Then what?" she asked.

John laughed. "We'll thank him for his interest in our election and make it clear that he should do his consulting somewhere else."

BG, reading a magazine, looked up. "His name is Jakob Warsaw. I just read that he may be America's next secretary of the Treasury. I told you John, Hinda was bullshitting."

John stopped smiling. He said he had forgotten a meeting, typed a message on his cell phone and ran off the ship.

CHAPTER 27

At the port, Mayer explained to Jake that because of the traffic, the high speed train was the best way back to his hotel. When one arrived, they said good-bye.

Jake followed a group of playful children up the steps onto the railroad car. They had come from the beach in their bathing suits. A teenaged girl with hair braided in cornrows came into their car and saw the laughing children.

"Look at those seats!" she said to them. "They're all wet. Dry them and sit on your towels."

The children quickly obeyed and continued their play.

The teenager said to the well-groomed American, "You look like a visitor. Can I help you?"

"I'm going to the Pacific Hotel."

"I work a few miles past there. It's about five or six stops from here. I'll show you."

"Are these kids by themselves?" Jake asked.

The teenager asked the children, "Who's with you? Where are you from?"

"Biko Village. They let us come by ourselves if we pass the swim test," one said.

The teenager explained, "It's a home for orphans. Where are you from?"

"America. Are they safe?"

"For sure," said the teenager. "Here everybody watches out for our little people."

"Did you say that you work near my hotel?" he asked.

"It's called Ahuva. If you have time, you should try to visit," she said.

"It's worth a special trip?"

"I think so. Our most innovative schools are there. It's rumored that one is working with the United States on cyber-warfare systems. At another, they built a GPS system where cars operate without drivers. The students at our famous school for music and arts act like they own the city. The musicians constantly surprise with impromptu performances at parks, shopping centers, hospitals, anywhere. And the artists covered buildings and playgrounds with graffiti."

"What kind of work do you do there?"

"On Friday and Saturday, I'm a 'Shabbos goy.' The religious people in this town don't work or carry things during the Sabbath. They pay me to do things they're not permitted to do. During the week, I'm working with a French company on genome research."

Jake was curious about the way she was dressed. She wore a long-sleeved blouse, stockings and a long skirt. "Do you have to wear certain clothes?"

"Not really. They want the women to dress modestly. I try to respect their customs."

The train passed a vast farm with several brightly colored buildings and tents. The teenager explained, "That is one of our new villages. They are modeled after a Burundi development. If we have another Ebola outbreak, like we had a few years ago, people with symptoms will be quarantined and treated there. The teachers and students built the clinic and the farms."

The train came to a stop. There was a loud noise as it hooked up with another railcar. Suddenly the room filled with an unpleasant odor.

Jake had to ask, "What the hell is that?"

"We have a research project with Ghana's Nkrumah University," the teenager explained. "Human waste from hundreds of toilets and latrines is going to a refinery where it's being made into some kind of product."

"I picked the wrong train," Jake said.

"The train is good. You may have picked the wrong time."

When Jake got off the train at the hotel, he picked up a soccer ball that had come to rest in his path. He saw two men who apparently were playing with it and threw the ball to them.

One waved thanks and kicked it to the other player, who then abruptly stopped. The man pulled out John's picture of

A Developing Country

Jake, and signaled his playing partner to look at Jake, pointing to the man walking toward the hotel. He then ran to a van with a BG logo. His friend ran to Jake, staying about twenty feet behind him.

As the van and Jake approached the entrance to the hotel, the door of the van opened, and the man following Jake approached, planning to overtake him.

Just then a group of people leaving the hotel blocked the BG men from reaching Jake, who, oblivious to the threat, walked into the lobby.

CHAPTER
28

In his hotel room, Jake found a gift-wrapped package on his bed. JM's message on the room phone explained it. "Thanks for your help Jake. Ruth's doctor told me she'll be all right. I told the front desk to put the IPhone in your room. It's the gift we were going to give the president tonight at his house. I hope you have success in your search."

Jake poured some whiskey and went on the balcony. He thought about the people he had observed since his arrival. They were more interesting than he ever imagined Africans would be. For the first time, he considered the possibility that he could actually live in this country but quickly dismissed the idea. It may have been possible when he was younger, living here with someone like Hinda. He was sure she would come to America. She would be impressed with his powerful friends. JM could get them invited to a dinner at the White House. A noise in the hall ended his reverie

Back inside his room he laid out a shirt, tie and a handkerchief for his jacket. He would be dressed well for the dinner with the president.

CHAPTER 29

When Jake left the taxi at the president's home, he saw that most of the guests were wearing casual clothes. He was more surprised to see a single guard at the gate ignoring the visitors and talking on a phone. He waited for some security check from her, but she only smiled and waved him into the compound.

Most of the people were standing alongside the simple arrangement of tables or near the bandstand. Many were dancing. When the music stopped, Hinda came over to Jake with her dance partner an old blind man.

"Judge Freeman, say hello to Jakob Warsaw," she said.

Jake shook the blind man's extended hand.

"Hinda tells me you traveled here with Mr. Mitchell. He and his wife have always been here when we needed them," the judge said.

"My closest friends," Jake said.

"Have you heard anything more about Ruth?" the judge asked.

"Only that her doctor told Mr. Mitchell that she'll be okay," Jake said.

Hinda led them to a table, where the judge and his aide sat with some of the judge's friends. Then she took Jake to a table with several people including the journalist and his wife, Mary, and a large man in a military uniform. She kissed Mary and hugged the Minister of Defense, General Nemonah.

When Jake showed Hinda the IPhone gift he brought for the president, Hinda said, "I suggest you let me give it to him. He's not himself tonight."

Hinda's son Stefen was talking to the president, when Hinda gave the president Jake's package.

"This is from the American. His name is Jakob Warsaw," she said.

The president did not look at Jake when he gave the gift to Stefen to open. "The American? What is it?" the president asked.

"A computer," Stefan said.

"You know how to work it?" the president asked.

"I'll figure it out."

"I can't use it. You want it?"

"Yes. Thank you!" Stefan said.

"When you're older," the president said. "He's an American?"

Guests gathered at Jake's table. Waiters brought platters of food. Beer, wine and other drinks were already cooling in buckets near the tables. Jake smiled when he saw one of the women servers slap Mkeeba after he fondled her. He reached for some vegetables and then stopped when the couple to his right bowed their heads and said grace.

The journalist's wife told a brief history of Bessedelya under the presidency of Simba. She mentioned BG and Ali as the candidates who had the best chances of succeeding the old president.

The journalist turned to Defense Minister Nemonah. "Suppose BG wins the election, could you take orders from him?"

"I may have to resign," Nemonah said. "He has never had to work with military advisors. Like many elected people, he may believe that he has the wisdom to go with his new power."

"Is it about not having military training?"

"It's about judgement. Can he listen to people who don't have his education?" Nemonah asked. "He has no experience. I'm afraid that for BG, diplomacy would be an excuse for not taking strong action."

"Our people must be protected. He follows laws that must be enforced, General. What else is there to consider?"

"Our border patrols confront families who want to escape from threats or are desperate to find work. I'm afraid BG lacks the morals a president should have in keeping out some of these people."

"That's a pretty heavy criticism," the journalist said. "We know he served as a missionary, and he is reputed to be a good family man."

"He may be very educated, but he does not believe what is clearly written in the Bible. He wants to let some *homos* run for important positions in my church," Nemonah explained. "Someone asked him why he would not let a married man who had committed adultery run for the office, but he would accept a man who left his wife to sleep with another man. He had no answer.

Hinda walked over with her son Stefen and a few of his friends. Jake stood, shook their hands, and then asked the minister, "Could you see Hinda as president?"

"No way. Hinda is not a politician. She doesn't respect power. She thinks you must always tell the truth. But I will say this about her. She treats everybody the same, like shit." He laughed. "Besides, the commander of our soldiers must have cajones. Something she's missing." He patted Hinda's behind.

She slapped his hand. "If you watched anything on television besides football, you'd know that women are taking over the world. Soon they'll be giving you orders."

Jake looked at Hinda. "Are you prepared to run the country?"

"I'd rather die," she said.

"Just until you start to feel sick?" Jake asked.

Hinda said to the children, "Mr. Warsaw is an American. He knows all the famous people you see on television."

"You know any football players?" one asked.

"Only Washington Redskins," Jake said.

"Redskins?" another child asked.

And someone else asked, "You know how to play any sports?"

"I was good with a saber," Jake said, "sword fighting." He stood up, took a knife from the table and struck a pose.

A Developing Country

The spectators were fascinated until the journalist pointed to one of the children wearing a leotard and said, "Isn't that what you wear when you're sword fighting?"

"Exactly," Jake said to great laughter.

A Falasha woman approached the president. She kissed him and turned to the guests. "Mr. President, everyone has made us feel welcome. We can never repay your many kindnesses. Our simple gift to you is some music from our country."

Ten people from her group joined her, and the Falasha boy near Jake ran to them.

Stefan walked over to the president. "You said I could have the computer when I was older. I'm older now."

The president gave him the IPhone.

"We caught some poachers today," the president said. "They killed some gorillas, but we saved a baby. He's at a zoo hospital. You want to see him?"

"Yeah, can I take some friends?" he asked.

"Okay. Ask the American if he wants to go," the president said.

Jake was dancing with Hinda when her son told him of the president's invitation.

"Tell him I'd like very much to go. Are you coming?" he asked Hinda.

"I wasn't invited," she answered.

CHAPTER
30

The children filled the SUV before the president got in the car. Jake squeezed into the backseat.

The children were at ease talking to the president. "I don't want to see the baby if he's hurt. Why did people kill his parents?" they asked.

"They get a lot of money for its body. They make medicines for sick people and for old people," the president said.

"You're old. Are you going to die soon?" asked one child.

"Yes," he said.

"I wish I could get the parts to make you live longer," said another.

"You would have to kill an animal. What would you tell its mother?" the president asked.

"I would tell her you are more important. She can have more children," said another.

"Not more important to the parents. They would die before they would give up their child," he said.

A Developing Country

Through the windshield, President Simba and Jake saw two people on a motor bike. The passenger on the back of the bike threw some trash in the road. The president accelerated, passed them and forced them off the road.

The bikers lay dazed on the ground when the president jumped out of the car and began berating them about the trash. When he grabbed the woman, the man wrestled her free and pushed the president away.

They got on their bike and began to ride away until the president poked a branch into their spokes making them fall over.

The angry driver pushed the president into a tree, where he fell to the ground bleeding from a cut on his forehead. The bikers then went to help the wild old man.

Jake, shocked by the scene, got out from under the screaming children and started running to the bikers who were trying to lift the president to his feet. Jake was almost hit by a car driven by Mkeeba who stopped and jumped out of his car. Jake watched stupefied, as the bodyguard shot the two people he must have thought were assaulting the president.

Jake stared at the two lifeless bodies until Mkeeba told him to help put the president in his car. He then told Jake to follow him in the car full of children. When Jake explained that he could not drive the president's standard transmission, Mkeeba told him to drive his car and to follow him.

The unconscious, bloody president leaned against Jake the entire drive to a prefabricated clinic, whose benefactors, according to a sign, were Ruth and Joshua Mitchell. Apparently Mkeeba had called ahead, and two nurses with a gurney were waiting. Jake stayed with the children in the other car and tried to calm them. He was surprised to see Hinda drive up and rush inside.

Twenty minutes later, she emerged from the clinic. She saw the blood on Jake's clothes and said, "You need some attention."

"It's the president's blood. How is he?" he asked.

"He's raising hell about something stupid, trash or junk in the road. He'll be all right. Mkeeba will stay with him tonight. I'll take the children home. When the nurse is finished, she'll take you back to the hotel."

Jake realized that Hinda was unaware of the shocking incident that had taken place an hour ago.

"I've arranged for you to meet the judge tomorrow to talk about Eedel. He has a trial in a town about an hour from here. Take a taxi and meet me here in the morning, Okay?"

"Is it so strange that I look like someone in Africa?" Jake asked still upset and confused, "And what about the bikers?"

Hinda appeared not to have heard his last question. "Something is upsetting the president. The judge has known him since they were young. Maybe he can explain why now that name seems to trouble him so much."

CHAPTER 31

Driving to meet the judge, Hinda pointed out that most of the homes they were passing had solar panels, satellite dishes and pans used to collect rainwater. Jake was not interested in the information.

"How did you learn about the president so quickly?" he asked.

"If anyone is involved in a violent crime or a hate crime, I expect to be notified immediately," she explained.

"A few hours ago, two people were executed for throwing trash on the ground," Jake said.

"That was a tragedy. We will help the bikers' families and punish the killer."

"Can you think of any civilized country that does not permit an accused man a trial?"

"We know our system is not perfect," she said.

"Not perfect? I'm talking about using deadly force on two vandals."

"We may have the safest streets and schools in the world. Can you say that about your country?"

"Are you saying the ends justify the means?"

"I'm telling you that most people, intent on hurting someone, hesitate when they know the punishment is death. Last night our system failed.

"Can there be extenuating circumstances? Does a judge have the ability to show mercy?"

"Yes. There is an automatic appeal process before three judges."

"Last night I saw a bodyguard murder two people. He thought he was doing his job. Will he go free?"

"A court will decide his fate, but I believe Mkeeba and his family will be severely punished.

"Years ago our people decided that they would trust judges to determine who was the cause of a violent act. A person found guilty would be put to death. All his relatives would provide funds for the victim and all would be banished from the country. No money would be spent to rehabilitate the guilty person or for prison construction and staff.

"Our justice system is constantly criticized in our media and from our colleges. Too often, innocent people have been killed. But the majority of our people continue to believe that the certainty of a death penalty is a better deterrent than the threat of incarceration. If you have a better plan, come here. Persuade the people. If you get enough votes, you can change the system."

CHAPTER 32

The courtroom, only half-filled, was in a small building. Except for the judge, Hinda and Jake, everyone was naked. On one side, a five-man jury wore carved wooden masks. Hinda and Jake sat in the back.

"Aren't we overdressed?" Jake asked.

"In this village, they believe that white visitors with strange clothes brought a disease that nearly wiped out the entire tribe. Now they don't want white people or clothes in their town," Hinda said.

She walked over to a couple sitting nearby to learn about the trial and then returned to Jake. "The woman on trial believes she must leave her man because he can't give her children. He says it is her fault because he has children from his other wives. The judge says she can leave him but must return all his gifts. He gave them the name of a doctor who may be able to diagnose their problem."

After the session ended, Hinda talked to the judge and returned to Jake. "He suggests we meet at a campus near here. It's an artists' colony."

Jake asked, "Does the judge like to look at the pictures?"

"You are going to love it. They teach art and dance and music. It is such an interesting place. They are always coming up with new stuff. Some of it is terrific. Some of the music is too loud, and I can't understand half of what they are singing. And the art is, well I can't wait for you to see what they're doing," she said.

CHAPTER 33

The school was in a park setting. Hinda, Jake, the judge and his aide walked into a sculpture garden and sat near a fountain. Hinda asked if the judge wanted anything.

He said, "See if they have a pillow. The chairs here are too hard."

Ballet music played in the background. Jake asked, "How do you like this music?"

"I like Louie Armstrong and Billie Holliday better," the judge said as the aide returned with a cushion and some bottles of water.

"You are anxious to learn what I know about Eedel, but I'm not sure anybody ever knew much about him," the judge began. "I mean where he came from, his motivation, his demons. When our people were lost in the jungle, he simply appeared, took charge of us and protected our ragtag group. He enabled us to survive many difficult trials, and when he was joined by Bess, they led us to build our country.

"My personal story may help you better understand why the two of them were so important to so many of us. My family was suffering in Ethiopia when a miracle occurred. We were told that airplanes were coming to take us to Israel. Once there, our lives were truly wonderful.

"I was teaching when my best friends persuaded some of us to move to a new part of Africa to start our own country. It was a difficult decision, but we were young and idealistic. We had been resettled only a short time, when our neighbors seemed to go insane. We expected the rest of the world to bring an end to their savagery and madness, but we were ignored. All we could do was run and try to hide.

"I was lucky," the judge continued. "My students found me delirious with fever, dehydrated, near death. They carried me with them on their terrible journey. They had no destination. We were joined by other refugees fleeing the barbaric madmen. We were always thirsty, tormented by the heat and the insects and the constant fear of robbers and other desperate men.

"Somehow we arrived at the deserted military base that is now our capital. The young man in charge there was Eedel. His rules were simple. There could be no violence. Everyone shared whatever they brought. Everybody had a job however distasteful. The strong had to help the weak.

"We seldom saw the young man. He rarely spoke and never seemed to sleep. When we were frightened by sounds of gunfire or wild animals, he would go into the darkness, often alone, and the threat would go away.

"One night the surviving members of a girls' school arrived with their principal. She was a former student of mine named Bess. She and Eedel became inseparable. He would stand in the shadows, transfixed, as she inspired us to overcome what seemed insurmountable obstacles."

An old man and woman walked from a nearby building and stood at the fountain watching the judge speak. Hinda walked to them and asked if she could be of help. Then Hinda interrupted the judge and said, "Some folks would like to talk to you when you have some time."

"Yes? What is the problem?" he asked.

"Please excuse us your Honor," said the old man. "Will you have a few minutes later to advise us about a very important matter?"

"I'll take the time now," the judge said.

"I'm Izak Bantu, and this is my wife Eve. Your son and his family live across the road from us."

"By the river?" the judge asked.

"Yes," Izak answered. "A month ago, my grandson printed some hateful messages about the Chinese people who moved into our neighborhood. His mullah said their shrine was against the teachings of the Koran. There was vandalism and fighting. My grandson was found guilty of incitement and put to death. His mullah fled the country. Now all of us must pay the penalty for the child's crime."

"The sentence for that offense is taught in all the schools," the judge said. "We are our brothers' keepers."

"May I speak?" Eve asked. The judge nodded. "Yesterday we were told that everyone related to my grandchild must leave Bessedelya. You know our family. For twenty years, not one trouble with the law from any of us. My children are respected nurses and teachers. Must the whole family suffer for the crime of one member?"

"If it were not that kind of crime, the family could make restitution," the judge said. "In the case hate crimes, the law is clear. Your family should prepare to leave the country."

When the old couple left, the judge was quiet for a few moments and then said to his aide, "I must make water," and they walked to a nearby building.

Jake was outraged. "Do you think the punishment fit the crime?" he asked Hinda.

"I don't want to discuss it," she said and sat quietly until the judge returned.

The judge continued. "Back then we heard about military coups, religious jihads and tribal wars, but our little towns were growing steadily and without conflict.

"Every group was given its own land and water. Our regular town meetings were long because everyone could speak and criticize. Every village and city had marketplaces and festivals. We shared the costs of roads and electricity and machinery. Eedel made certain we located our towns in strategic places that could protect us from attacks. Bess insisted that we establish high standards for our institutions and have continuous oversight and transparency. Her schools were demanding of the teachers and available to everyone day and night.

"We ignored a rumor that two hundred miles from here, a general declared himself president of the region including what is now Bessedelya. He created and equipped a powerful palace guard and claimed control of many cities including ours. He began buying and building many extravagant things until he had used all the money provided by European and American countries.

"One of his officials sent an order that we must pay two million dollars. He said it was our fair share of taxes needed to run the country. Several of us went to the general to explain our financial position and to plead for relief. We were imprisoned and tortured. I was blinded.

"Finally he agreed to free us and wait for the money, but only if Eedel, Bess and their children would be his hostages. They did not hesitate to accept his offer. Before they were taken away, Bess suggested that Simba be left in charge until the next election. We were returned to our families and Bess, Eedel and their children were taken away.

"A few weeks later a dozen mutilated bodies were dumped in our town square. Badly burned, they were hardly recognizable. This beautiful couple had saved all of us when we had no hope to survive. Immediately and from all over, thousands came to our city. The peaceful villagers became an uncontrollable mob. They drove to the general's palace where they butchered him and his followers."

"What about their children? Did any survive?" Hinda asked.

The judge shook his head. "We couldn't tell if their girls were among the bodies. Bess had a special friend, Yochevet. She lives in the old-age home near the orange groves. She may have more information."

"I don't know that place," Hinda said.

"The one that has the Dr. Kay clinic," the judge said.

CHAPTER 34

Jake thought the trip to the assisted-living home was a waste of time. If Eedel's children were murdered, he could imagine no connection to the man he apparently looked like. At the entrance was a sign that read The Dr. Kay Clinic. It pointed to a small building with beautiful landscaping about two hundred yards away.

"Named for your Dr. Kevorkian," Hinda explained.

When they entered the lobby of the assisted living building, two women were yelling at each other until Hinda separated them. She looked at the register for Yochevet's room and then explained to Jake, "The Hutu nurse did not want to help the Watutsi visitor."

"I thought these disputes were settled?" asked Jake.

"For some the hatred will never end," Hinda said.

While walking down the hall, they passed many rooms with the doors open. They saw people watching TV or asleep.

A Developing Country

As they approached Yochevet's room, Jake walked ahead and peeked into the half-opened door. Inside he saw a couple making love. As he quickly backed out of the wrong room, he saw Hinda pointing to the next room.

In Yochevet's room they saw a woman sleeping in a chair. A dog at her feet looked up as Hinda gently touched the woman's hand. "Yochevet?"

The woman opened her eyes, looked at the empty bed, and pointed outside.

The beautiful grounds were crowded with residents and attendants and visitors. Hinda asked several people if they knew Yochevet. Finally one man got up from his chair and pointed to a group sitting under a very large tree.

Yochevet was teaching a foreign language using her hands to describe *little* and *large*. A young girl, breast-feeding her child, laughed at the sexual reference as Hinda and Jake stood watching.

"Excuse me," Hinda said. "I'm looking for Yochevet."

"Everyone calls me YoYo," said the teacher.

A woman holding a dog in her lap said, "You're the skinny one on the TV that shows the dirty stuff. I like your sex movies. I don't understand the poetry."

"What can I do for you?" asked YoYo.

"Please tell me what you remember about Eedel and Bess," Hinda said.

Jake saw YoYo's expression turn grim and then sad. She looked at him and then at Hinda. She put down her language cards and stared into space.

"We are here today because of them," she began. "Eedel was the man in charge. He would not explain or discuss. He did not like you to disagree. Only Bess could make him back down. Bess, Bess. Everybody loved her so much. I still hear her laughter. I don't think Eedel ever smiled until she came to us. Then he was a changed man. So many refugees were coming. They spoke different languages, had strange customs and religions. She told me how I could help them get settled, and why it was important that they save their traditions and music. How we should give special attention to the elders of each group, because they would remember their holy days and history. She was a wonderful teacher."

"Under my bed is a box," she said to Hinda. "Bring it to me." When Hinda ran to the room, YoYo looked at Jake. "Are you her father? Take off your glasses."

She didn't wait to look at Jake but instead looked back at Hinda going after the box and continued, as Jake put back his sunglasses. "Many people gathered in front of their little house. We begged them not to go. She sat on the porch feeding her baby boy; her daughters were at her feet. She was wearing a beautiful dashiki. She sang a song that told us not to be afraid.

"Eedel came out of the house. He said it was time. She asked me to come with her inside. She put perfume on the baby's heart, said it would help him live a sweet life."

"What happened to the baby?" Jake asked.

YoYo wasn't listening. "Bess filled a bag of things he should have. Food, pictures, clothes, some money and gave him to the president. The president drove away. We were all crying."

"But what happened to the baby?" Jake asked again.

"The president said he gave the baby and a lot of money to a Polish church group leaving for the United States."

A Developing Country

Jake's legs almost buckled when he connected the odd spelling of his name to the missionaries.

"For years we tried to find him. We sent people to America, but we never found the baby or the missionaries. I swear we tried."

Hinda had returned with the box and put it on the ground at her feet as YoYo was talking.

Yochevet picked up the box and opened it. She took out each picture and held it close to her face, mumbled something, and then placed it in a pile at the side of the box. Finally YoYo came to a picture that made her smile. There were nine people staring at the camera. A pregnant woman sat in the center with two girls by her side. YoYo and Hinda stared at the picture.

"That's me," YoYo said, pointing. "I was pretty, huh?"

"Not as pretty as you are now," Hinda said.

YoYo laughed at the compliment. "Look at the president, always next to Eedel, and that's Bess. Beautiful wasn't she? She had the baby not long after this picture."

Hinda gently took the picture to Jake. She pointed to the pregnant Bess and then to the president. The man next to the president looked exactly like Jake.

Jake was overwhelmed. He turned and walked inside into the lobby where he collapsed on a large padded chair.

Hinda put back the pictures, kissed Yochevet and rushed to find Jake.

Jake was staring at the floor when Hinda found him. She put her hands on his shoulders. He had been crying.

"You've had a big shock mister," she said.

"Visiting days at the orphanage were the worst for me. Everyone would be so excited. They'd scream when they recognized their parents' cars coming. Over the years my disappointment became hatred," he said.

"You couldn't have known then, but you know now. They were very special people. You found out you come from royalty," Hinda said. "I think this discovery calls for a celebration. What do you think?"

"I think I want to be left alone. Take me back to my hotel."

"I've got a better idea. An escape your rich friends love, a few hours in Fun City. We'll come back whenever you're ready."

CHAPTER 35

As they drove to a small private airport, Hinda was concerned with Jake's silence.

"The place where your parents are buried is not out of the way if you'd like to visit," Hinda said.

"Yes I'd like that," Jake said.

When they passed the baseball stadium where her son played, Jake saw the cemetery. Hinda parked.

They entered far from the area where Jake had taken water from the friendly lady. As they walked, Hinda pointed to graves of the pioneers who built the country. There were no monuments. Finally they came to a plain stone with the inscription *Our Beloved Founders* and the names *Bess, Eedel, Clara and Esther.*

"I was their son, their brother. When we played together, what was the name they called me?" Jake wondered.

As he stared at the pots of flowers by his family's grave, Jake was surprised by how emotional he became and how comforted he was when Hinda held his arm.

CHAPTER 36

It was a short trip to the airport. Hinda waved to some pilots eating at the grill and then sat down to file her flight plan. When she walked away, Jake saw a man look at her destination plan and make a call.

Hinda went through the necessary checklist before starting her plane's twin engines. Jake tried hard to conceal his fear of flying as she drove down the runway and up into the clouds.

"You have a dream. You know how to get things done. Why not run for office?" Jake was trying to ignore the flashes of lightning.

"I hate the campaigns. I can't explain the issues in sixty-seconds, and I hate the compromises.

"Don't you see how much more effective you'll be, when you become the leader of your country," Jake said.

"Our country, Jake," she corrected. "With your help we will make Africa a superpower."

CHAPTER 37

At the Fun City airport, Hinda was recognized by two mechanics coming from the terminal. Hinda checked in, and then she and Jake went outside to get a shuttle to the casino. As they were about to get on a bus, one of the mechanics came running to them.

"When we went out to the field, we saw a mechanic from BG's group climbing into the cockpit of your plane," he said. "She was surprised when I stopped her before she went to work on the fuel line. She mumbled something about thinking this was what she was told to do, but then she climbed down and hurried away. I've never seen her before. It was weird. BG's planes park on the other side of the field."

"That is strange," Hinda said. "Thanks, thanks a lot."

The huge lobby of the Fun City casino was unusually crowded when Hinda and Jake arrived. Two young girls, followed by their fashionably dressed mother, ran to Hinda.

"These pretty ladies belong to Mrs. Ali Mohammed. You've met Dinna. This is Jake Warsaw," Hinda said.

"Your husband has been a most considerate host," Jake said.

"He told me about your search. I hope it will be successful," she said as the girls pulled at her skirt. "My girls are afraid the stores will run out of clothes before they get there."

"Come with us Hinda," Dinna said.

"Maybe later," Hinda said.

The crowds around the craps tables were noisy, and all the different games were busy. Hinda saw a familiar face at one of the cashiers' windows. She thought Jake would like to meet the distinguished man taking chips from his pockets to cash in. She escorted Jake over to him.

"This fortunate man is one of your ambassadors, Martin Lowell Miller," Hinda said.

"And this man may be the next secretary of the Treasury," Miller said, shaking Jake's hand. "It would take somebody as strong as Jakob Warsaw to get you to Fun City."

"I heard they just built a nice library here," Hinda said. "I was looking for a book."

"Tonight I saw how affirmative action can work," Miller said. "The Europeans would not make room for me at several tables, until they needed a loser to fill their quota. An African American would do perfectly. When I was given the opportunity, I killed them."

"That's so interesting," Hinda said. "Let me just write that on my list of things I don't give a shit about."

A Developing Country

The ambassador saw a well-dressed man leading an entourage toward them. "I'm about to introduce you to President Mugabe one of the most powerful men in Africa."

But Mugabe spoke first. "Welcome, Mr. Jakob Warsaw." Jake shook his hand.

"You must honor us with your presence. When you finish gambling, join me on my yacht." He looked at Hinda. "Leave the hooker. We have others much younger."

Hinda slapped Mugabe and screamed, "You're a fucking animal."

Mugabe's bodyguard started to hit Hinda, but Jake pushed him away as the casino security guards quickly separated the group. Mugabe abruptly left with his people following him.

Hinda told Jake, "I'm going to find a bar. Stay here. We'll catch up later."

Jake started to follow her, but the ambassador grabbed his arm. "Wait a minute," he said. "She'll be okay. And you can't hurt Mugabe's feelings. If you want to see him, he's always at that big corner table. Talk to me for a minute." He asked a passing waiter to bring them drinks. "I'm glad you're here. We can use all the help we can get for the port vote."

"What do you care about wildlife preserves and fishing boats?" Jake asked.

"Is that all you've been told?"

"Not much more."

"We need a large facility at this location."

"Who's we?" Jake asked.

"The United States. The vote is about gaining permission to begin construction. Once the work's begun, we can incorporate the infrastructure and buildings we need."

"You're going too fast for me," Jake said.

"We don't care what kind of port they build. Our only interest is in the stability of this region. America needs a base of operations in this part of Africa."

"The president seems to be popular enough to keep getting reelected. Can't he get this project approved?"

"He's too unpredictable. Today he's supportive because we'll put up all the money. The next day he only wants to lecture us about our support of apartheid and dictators. There's too much at stake to leave it up to a confused old man. And you've seen how tough his granddaughter is. Hinda could get him to go the wrong way."

"His granddaughter? I thought she was his daughter."

Miller said, "I don't think so. The story I heard is that the president's daughter came home pregnant from some foreign country. When Hinda was a baby, her mother died. The president raised her with his other kids."

"What foreign country?"

"Wherever she'd been visiting, I guess. France, England, America," Miller said.

Jake was stunned by the thought that the beautiful woman in that delegation thirty-five years ago gave birth to Hinda, that he might be her father.

"Where are you going? I want to tell you about our plans," the ambassador said.

Jake didn't respond and left the casino. He walked into and out of several restaurants looking for Hinda. He passed through a line of people waiting to see a famous comedian and another crowd getting tickets to see a musical review.

Finally he spotted Hinda sitting in a restaurant by herself in front of a huge aquarium.

She was happy to see him. "You didn't play very long."

"I thought you'd stay and bring me some luck."

"I'm ready. Let's go," she said.

"It's too late," Jake said, taking out his wallet. "I've lost all my money."

"I can lend you some."

"Maybe later, there are lines trying to see some of the shows. Would you like to.."

"Slow down, Jake. I'll bet you haven't noticed how nice it is here."

"I was thinking."

"Stop thinking for a few minutes. Oh wait. I hope you're not upset with what happened in the casino. Mugabe's garbage."

"It's not that," he said. "It's something else."

"I look different. I bought myself a present. When I'm unhappy, I go shopping." She touched the hoop of her new earrings. "What do you think?"

"Nice," he said.

"They're not real. Come. Let me show you the beach. You'll love it." She called the waiter for her check.

Jake paid the man and caught up with Hinda as she pointed to a store that sold swimwear. She suggested they get bathing suits and change before going to the beach.

There were many people on blankets and a few swimming. A few came out of the water topless. Hinda led him to an abandoned blanket and sat down. "Here," she said. "Sit next to me." She took a joint from her shoulder bag. "If all else fails, I've got some stuff that will relax you."

Hinda looked beautiful in her bikini.

"Do you mind talking about yourself?" Jake asked.

"A background check before you try to get me in bed?" she asked.

"The tattoo."

"I'm not HIV positive. I was a flower child until I got my act together. My first real love urged me to get an education and helped me get into med school."

"Can you tell me about your family? Your parents?"

"Wow. You want a proctologic examination next?" She laughed. "Okay. I was very young when my mother died."

"Your father?"

"Never knew him."

Jake stood and then walked to the water, paused and walked back to Hinda. This would be the most difficult question he had ever asked. "Did she discuss her life before or when you were born?"

"She was fourteen and pregnant with me when she came from Somalia with a group of slaves. They were freed by the president. When my mother died, he raised me in his house with his other children."

Jake could not repress his sigh of relief. "Where'd you put that joint?" As they lit it, there was a sudden downpour with thunder and lightning.

CHAPTER 38

Jake and Hinda ran into the hotel lobby. Ali's wife and girls, now changed into their Moslem dress for their trip home, waved to Hinda, and she joined them. Jake walked up to the registration desk.

"When do you think the storm will blow over?" he asked.

"Tomorrow morning," the man at the desk said.

"I'd like two of your best rooms," Jake said.

"I'm sorry. I have nothing for tonight. There's a nice hotel.." he started to say.

"They have no rooms," Jake said as Hinda came alongside him.

Hinda, the celebrity, had been recognized by the bellhops who signaled the desk clerk.

"Not one?" Hinda asked.

"Just one," the clerk said.

As they entered their room, there was a loud noise and the building started to shake.

"Earthquake," Came a cry from the hallway.

"Hinda. Come on," Jake urged as he ran to the door.

"Go, Jake. I'll be right behind you." Earthquakes were common in Bessedelya, and she was not concerned with this one.

Outside it was a frightening scene with heavy rain and continuing bursts of lightning. Two retarded children were playing on the metal swings in the playground. Inside was a game room where a teenager was playing a video game. Jake joined some badly frightened guests who had run outside. He saw that they were terrified watching the endangered children. Then he heard one lady say she noticed the babysitter in the game room.

"Aren't you supposed to be watching those kids?" someone yelled at the girl in the room.

"I told them to come in. They won't listen," the sitter said without moving.

Jake ran to the children. He dragged them to the safety of the building moments before lightning struck the playground. Jake saw that the babysitter didn't look up until she felt the wet children hugging her. One of the guests told Jake that he would be blessed for that good deed.

The rain stopped. Jake walked upstairs to the room and saw Hinda asleep in the bed. When he got out of his wet clothes and came out of the bathroom, she was awake and waiting for him.

Jake had never experienced the passion he felt that night.

After they made love Jake said, "Will you come to America with me?"

"Could I have a house at the beach and one in the city and a housekeeper?" she asked.

"I'm not playing with you," Jake said.

"You should know I wouldn't be happy there."

"What could I offer you that would make you happy?"

"An African address."

He saw she was serious. Jake did not know what to say.

Admiring hotel employees stopped Hinda as Jake went to check out. She entered the gift shop, purchased an item and a newspaper and rejoined Jake. He took the paper, looked at his name in the headlines and opened Hinda's gift. It was a passport wallet.

"What's this for?" asked Jake.

"You said yours was empty. Maybe mine will bring you luck."

CHAPTER 39

It was perfect flying weather. Hinda grew excited when she pointed through the clouds to coral beds and small islands along the coast.

"Why all the small dams?"

"It's the cheapest way to get electricity to our remote areas," Hinda said.

Jake was unimpressed. "We got power to rural farms a hundred years ago."

"In those buildings are laboratories creating seeds that grow in terrible soil and climate. We'll be able to feed millions," Hinda said.

"When you come with me to America, I'll get scientists to do everything you want to do."

"Can they do this?" She left the controls and climbed into the backseat. "Look! No hands."

Jake couldn't believe what she did. "Are you crazy? Get your ass back here."

A Developing Country

Hinda returned to her seat and kissed his terrorized face. "You're safe with me, Mr. Warsaw. Look down there. I really believe creation was interrupted here, right here. Some say this was once the Garden of Eden. I don't know about that, but if where we live emerged from the ocean, there must be many wonders that never rose from the bottom. If Africa is where it all began, a united Africa may be how to finish God's work."

Their plane arrived and taxied to a halt. Hinda and Jake sat silently. Both had much to think about.

CHAPTER 40

They checked in at the terminal, took their bags to Hinda's car and left the airport. Jake noticed a BG van following them.

Hinda's house was in a residential area with small, functional and modern homes.

"I've got to leave something for my housekeeper. Want to come in?" The front door was not locked. Hinda put some money under the salt shaker on the kitchen table. "Want a drink?"

"I want to hold you," Jake said.

Hinda led Jake into her bedroom. After the passionate sex Hinda whispered. "You've made me fall in love again. How am I going to make it after you leave tomorrow?"

When they were dressed and prepared to leave, the front door opened. The housekeeper entered, leading a tall, thin man with a vacant expression.

"We just had a nice walk, Dr. Raisal," the housekeeper said, hugging Hinda. "Are we going to have company for supper?"

"No. Just fix for you and Aaron. This is Mr. Warsaw, Lilah. Jake, Lilah is my most important friend. I couldn't function without her. Aaron is my husband. Isn't he handsome?"

Her husband showed no recognition when Hinda hugged him and kissed him on the cheek. "I think it's time for a haircut big guy," she said. "See you later."

When they left her house, Hinda looked at Jake and then at her IPhone messages and then at Jake again.

"Aaron is an engineer," she said. "He was in Rwanda working with the Tutsis when the Hutus' massacre started. He wasn't able to leave. He witnessed the atrocities every day, for weeks. Arms and legs and noses cut off children. He called me at night crying. Finally he stopped calling. He'd lost his mind. We've tried many treatments. So far, nothing has helped."

She paused. "The president left me a message. He wants to see you. He's visiting the family of one of the terrorists' bomb victims. I'll drop you at your hotel and let you know when I get the address where you can meet him." She dialed another number. "We'll go as soon as I make this call.

"You're not coming with me?" asked Jake.

"I must meet some leaders of our organization." She kissed Jake. "I'll catch up with you later."

CHAPTER 41

A number of visitors were waiting to pay their respects to the parents of the victim. A BG man, who had followed Jake in a truck, watched the American extend his condolences. Then the bereaved couple pointed Jake to an old man sitting on a glider on the side of the house.

The president was staring at a bulldozer grading a building site in the housing development across the street. He held a newspaper with Jake's picture on the front page.

The president smiled when he saw Jake. "I was afraid you were Eedel. You see, before they took him away, he told the Congress that he thought I should be the president until he came back or until the elections in a few months. Nobody objected except me. I told him I didn't know what to do. He said, 'If the country is ever in trouble, serious trouble, I'll be there for you.' When I saw you, I thought something bad was going to happen and Eedel's come back to help me. I got very scared."

"You thought Eedel returned?" Jake asked, confused.

A Developing Country

"You look exactly like him. But when you came to my house, I was told you call yourself an American. I realized you couldn't be his blood," the president explained. "Eedel would never say that. He was an African."

"I'm called an African American," Jake said.

"We know black people have become powerful in America. We see that. But you Americans have no real interest in our world. Oh, you sometimes spend a few hours getting your picture taken holding our children, speaking with the leaders. But in your heart, you are not African."

"That's not fair. We use our influence, send billions of dollars."

"But not your children. You come for a visit, but you don't come here to live. You don't bring us your knowledge or your experience. You see, Mr. Warsaw, we have so much to do, and we need leaders like Eedel. If you were his blood, you would be here."

A lady came and told the president that everyone was waiting for him to sit down and eat. She said there was a place at the table for Jake, but Jake said he had to prepare to leave the next morning.

"Tell your taxi to stop by the Kwanzaa a few miles from here," the president said. "Let me know about Mr. Mitchell's wife when you hear something."

"I was expecting to see Hinda before I left," Jake said.

"It's early. You go and enjoy the festival. She'll come here, and I'll tell her where you'll be."

CHAPTER 42

At the Kwanzaa, the streets and sidewalks were crowded. Jake started to make some calls but noticed his cell phone battery was low. When he saw a building with a Travelers' Aid sign, he told the driver to stop. He wanted a quiet place to call his office, to confirm the time he would be picked up in the morning and to try to reach Hinda.

The BG man who followed Jake when he left the president had picked up another BG employee. When they saw Jake enter the building, they parked nearby and called their office.

"We got him," one said.

"Don't do anything until you hear from me. John sent out the word to hold up," the office man said.

"Forget about it. I've got that thousand spent," the man in the car said as he hung up.

On the porch of the building, a teenage girl was doing her homework. She did not seem to notice the screams from inside the house, but she smiled at Jake when he walked in the door.

Two young boys were wrestling next to an overturned chair. Laughing, they looked up from under a table at him.

From a back room a voice yelled, "When your father comes home, you're going to get a whipping you'll never forget."

Still on the floor, one of the boys said, "Welcome. Are you thirsty?"

"No thank you. I need a charger," Jake said.

One of the boys got up, took Jake's hand, pointed to a bathroom and then went back to play. Jake laughed.

He started down the hall where he saw a room with beds separated by curtains. Two women were ministering to an old lady visible behind one of the curtains. One of the two women, in a nurse's uniform, stopped Jake and said, "Please wait in the front room. Someone will be with you in about five minutes."

The boys were watching television. One asked Jake, "Do you want some food? We have juice and cheese and some fried fish in the refrigerator."

"I'm not hungry thank you. What do you charge? What's the cost?" Jake asked.

The boys looked surprised at the question. "It's what we do," one said. "Didn't you see the sign?"

Jake was impressed with the children's response. "I'd like to leave something for the manager." On his way out, he put a fifty-dollar bill in a bowl of candy on a desk and waved to the children as they turned to watch TV.

Jake didn't see the mother return, catch one of the boys before he could run away and smack the other one. Through their tears, they managed to show her the money left by Jake. She wrote a note and gave it and the money to one of the boys. "Give this back to the man who left it, and then come right back. Do you hear me?" The boy ran out of the house but turned in a different direction than the man who left the money.

Jake walked aimlessly, inspecting the various pushcarts and window displays. At one place he bought some palm wine, and at another he bought some marijuana. He found a table near some street musicians, lit the joint and sat watching the passersby.

The music reminded him of the sounds at the airport when he arrived. The sights of the past few days started running through his mind. Old people walking and holding hands, modern buildings under construction everywhere, crowded farmers' markets, the participation at the speakers' corners, the pride in their country.

Jake bought some more wine. He noticed some people dancing in the street a few blocks away and started to join them, when he heard someone call his name.

"Mr. Warsaw. I'd like you to meet my family." At a long table, BG Jr. pointed to his wife and children as he called their names. "Mr. Warsaw is the son of Bess and Edel, yes the founders of our country." The children stood to shake Jake's hand.

Jake said, "In my short time here, I've only heard high praise of you and your family. Good luck in the election."

Jake continued down the street, when he saw another familiar face. He started to greet the family sitting with the pretty woman when he realized she was the sex worker who gave him the massage. He abruptly turned at the next corner and hurried until he was next to a bandstand.

A Developing Country

The music and the exuberant dancers were wonderful, but he was starting to feel dizzy. He leaned against a tree and then sat among some spectators. Two girls appeared and pulled him to his feet. In a moment he was holding their hands and dancing with others in a wide circle.

When the music stopped, he stumbled through the crowd and held on to a car to catch his breath. Jake watched the two girls run to a pickup truck that slowed to wait for them. They waved to him to come with them. As the truck got closer, Jake was shocked to realize the driver and his familiar passengers were Eedel, Bess and his sisters.

The boy from the Travelers Aid had caught a glimpse of Jake and stopped to rest. Just as he sat, he saw Jake run after the pickup truck. He followed for a few blocks and then had to sit down.

Jake was exhausted. He slowly walked past an alley.

Two men in BG uniforms were waiting for him. One pulled him into the alley and the other hit him on the head knocking him to his knees. The first man took out a knife and stabbed the semiconscious victim.

Jake felt the knife cut into his arm, and then the pain struck as it hit his chest.

"John said scare him not kill him," his BG partner said. He took cash from Jake's wallet, threw the wallet to the side, helped drag Jake back into the shadows of the alley and then ran away.

A few minutes later, Jake heard the voice of a little boy.

"Mister," the boy said. "I have something for you."

"Get the hell out of here," the BG man yelled.

Ignoring the BG man's threat, the boy took out the note and read, "Dear visitor, Thank you for your gift. I'm sure you did not intend so much. Please come again." The boy walked forward with the note and money, until he saw the glint of the knife blade and then ran out of the alley.

The BG man's hand covered Jake's mouth, and again Jake felt himself being dragged back against a wall where he was told, "Don't move."

Suddenly an old policeman and a young policewoman were standing at the entrance of the alley. The little boy was by their side. The BG man dropped the knife and kicked it away.

"What's going on here?" the old policeman asked.

"He gave me money, begged me to bugger him. He wanted a white Christmas." The BG man laughed.

The young policewoman then asked Jake, "Did you pay him to have sex with you?"

"No," Jake mumbled.

"Why are you back there on the ground?" she asked.

"He had a knife," Jake said.

The old policeman asked, "Did you put a knife on him?"

"He's lying. I don't carry a knife."

The little boy had picked up the knife and was looking at it when the policeman took it from him and showed it to the policewoman. He also picked up the blood-stained wallet.

The policewoman took the knife and showed it to the BG man. "Is this yours?"

"No way," he answered.

The policeman noticed that the BG man had a sheath on his belt and told the policewoman to see if the knife fit the sheath. It did. He asked Jake if the wallet was his. Jake nodded.

She looked to her partner for instructions. They walked back several steps. He put his arm around her shoulders as he talked to her. She seemed to resist his order, but he appeared unmoved as he ushered the spectators out of the alley.

"What is your name?" she asked as she took out her gun.

"I ain't done nothing. My name's Heller. Albert Heller."

"Albert Heller, you are guilty of a violent crime." She looked back at the officer.

"Do you have anything to say to the victim?" she asked.

"He propositioned me," he insisted.

"Before I execute judgment, do you want to give me the name of your family?" she asked in an unsteady voice.

"Execute hell, I want a lawyer. Call John at the BG Company." He gave her a BG business card.

From her behavior, it was apparent this was the first time the policewoman had fired her gun at a living human being. She was shaking as she shot and killed the BG man.

The policeman checked Heller and saw that he was dead. He started to lift Jake and noticed his bloody shirt. "We'll get you to a doctor. Do you have a car? Do you live near here? Can I call someone for you?"

Jake shook his head.

Driving to the hospital, Jake tried to comfort the policewoman. She was still crying when she helped him out of the police car and into the emergency room where a doctor was waiting.

"The policewoman showed me your bloody wallet," the doctor said as he cleaned the wound and gave Jake medication. "You are a lucky man. It saved your life."

Jake passed out. When he awoke three doctors were looking down at him. One of them said, "Since I moved from Chicago, believe it or not, this is the first mugging I've seen."

CHAPTER 43

Back in his hotel room, Jake dropped his clothes on the floor and turned on the shower. He stood in the hot water crying. He remembered when he was almost raped by two big boys at his foster home.

Afterward he dressed and then sat on the bed unable to move. Finally he began to pack a few things. He poured a half glass of whiskey, turned on the television, flipped some channels and then turned it off. He went out on the balcony came back in and finished packing.

He sat in a chair for several hours and then went into the bathroom and washed his face and hands. He turned on the television changing channels until he saw Hinda in front of a picture of the poet Derek Walcott.

She was reading, "I'm just a red nigger who loves the sea. I had a sound colonial education. I have Dutch, nigger, and English in me. And either I'm a nobody, or I'm a nation."

"A nobody or a nation, a nobody or a nation," Jake repeated.

He hit the phone message button and heard, "Mort Plant here, Mrs. Carver's AA. Bad news and good news. You will not be Treasury secretary, but the president was impressed with your list of supporters. He wants to meet you next week."

Jake went to the next message. It was Hinda. "Please call me. I'll get to the hotel before you leave. Let me know that you're all right, please."

Jake was dozing by his luggage when his wakeup call rang at five in the morning.

A bellhop picked up his bags, and Jake checked out. Ali and his driver were talking outside the entrance. He saw Dinna in pink leotards sleeping in the back with her little dog.

On the road to the airport they stopped behind a school bus. "Dinna is a student here. Her first class is at eight. We were lucky she didn't get the night schedule classes."

Jake interrupted. "I'm sorry, Ali. I don't feel like talking."

As they approached the bridge, Jake was reminded that he would soon be leaving. He regretted having booked so early a flight. He had expected to be with Hinda last night. The medicine made him drowsy and confused. In what seemed like a few minutes, they were at the airport and inside the terminal.

CHAPTER 44

J](#)**ake started to call Hinda** but was distracted and forgot, when Ali took his plane ticket and passport and told Dinna to wait with him. Dinna and her dog followed Jake into a duty-free shop.

The only saleswoman was with a customer. A very old man was sleeping in a chair. Jake saw that the newspaper he was reading had fallen to the floor. When he picked it up, he saw the headline *Son of Eedel and Bess Visiting*. Before he could read more, the old man woke.

He looked at Jake, blinked and said, "What took you so long?"

The saleswoman, free of the other customer, said, "Thank you, Dad. I can help the gentleman now," and then to Jake," Something for your wife or child?"

Jake thought of Ruth, "For a lady in the hospital."

"Young? Old?"

Jake saw some scarves he liked. He told the saleslady, "Pick out a few for me," and then, "Dinna pick some for your mother and sister."

"Good choice," the saleslady said. "You also may want to consider some wonderful French perfume maybe for your secretary?"

"Anything made in Africa?" he asked.

"Yes, but not the same quality," she said, reaching behind herself. "This is produced not far from here."

When she turned around, she was holding a blue bottle. Jake stared in disbelief. He wondered if it had the same scent that his mother had rubbed on him. He paid for three bottles of the perfume, and he asked her to wrap all the gifts but one. He put one of the blue bottles in his pocket. While she was wrapping, they saw Ali running toward them.

"You must board the plane right away," Ali said.

"I have a few packages," said Jake.

"Leave them," Ali said as he pulled Jake out of the gift shop. "I'll pick them up later and ship them to you. I just heard some shocking news. William Gee and his family have fled the country. The terrorist they captured said John was financing their work to discredit me. What the hell was he thinking?"

Jake was too sore from the mugging and groggy from the painkillers to grasp the significance of Ali's news. He hugged Dinna and Ali and then headed to the departure area. He had forgotten to call Hinda.

A Developing Country

In the Rome airport, Jake entered the long security line. The woman checking credentials looked like the policewoman who had driven him to the hospital. Jake started trembling. He smelled Albert Heller's hand on his face. Tears came to his eyes as he pushed the tray with his things to the conveyor.

In front of him, he saw the security guard show a little old white lady how to raise her hands above her head in the X-ray machine. After they told her she could go through, she asked angrily, "Did you see anything hidden in my coochie?"

The inspector did not smile.

As the plane took off for America, Jake overheard two men who had boarded with him in Bessedelya.

"I can't get over that place," one said. "Reminds me of when I first saw Cuba, the people, the potential, but you know, Bessedelya's so much more advanced. One day it's going to be big."

"It's still Africa. Nobody's rushing to live in a developing country"

Jake affixed his seat belt, took out the blue bottle of perfume and opened it. The fragrance was strangely comforting.

CHAPTER 45

The cold shocked Jake as he carried his bags from the Dulles terminal to Becky's car. After a warm greeting, he told her about Ruth and why he could not wait to learn her condition. He called JM.

"How's Ruth?" he asked.

"Mean as ever. Ask her yourself."

"Welcome home, Jakob," Ruth said.

"Are you feeling okay? You sound tired," Jake said.

"I can't wait to hear all about your trip."

"I'll tell you everything in the morning. What did the doctors say?"

"I want to hear about you and Hinda," Ruth said.

"Come on, Ruthie. What did they say?"

"They want to try a new protocol."

"Great. This time they'll."

Ruth cut him off. "Please, Jake. To me it's the same medicine from different bottles. They give me poison or burn me with radiation after they cut me. I can't go through it anymore. And it's not just me. Josh, our children, you, everybody I love suffers with me. It's enough. I've decided to go to a hospice. They'll keep me comfortable."

Jake wasn't prepared for this news. "A hospice? When? Where?"

"Come visit," she said. "We'll talk."

Becky was in good spirits as they drove away. "Glad the cannibals left something for me to eat. I missed you a lot. Bermuda was fabulous. A photographer told me I may make a section in the *Sunday Times*. Are you as exhausted as you look? Want to stop for a drink or something to eat?"

"Okay," he said, still reeling from Ruth's decision.

"Okay coffee or okay a bar?"

"Maybe some coffee."

Becky pulled into the parking lot of a diner. Tinsel and plastic Christmas trees were in the windows. A number of young couples in tuxedos and gowns were leaving the restaurant. Dirty dishes on several of the tables were ignored by the two waitresses talking to the three policemen sitting at the counter. One waitress got up, came to Jake and Becky's booth and took their order.

Becky noticed a black man eating at a table across the room. She watched him get up and move to a table that had not been cleared of dishes. He began eating the food left in the plates and drinking from the glasses. Becky was sickened by the scene.

"Oh Jesus, I'm going to throw up," she said.

"What's the matter?"

"That guy over there. He's eating somebody's leftovers."

"I guess the service is slow," Jake joked.

The waitress brought their coffee and pastries and went back to the counter.

"It's not funny. He's a freak. Should we get the police to escort us to my car?" she asked.

Suddenly Jake was angry. "No napkin on his lap, eating with his fingers. The son of a bitch should have his hands cut off."

She was surprised at Jake's reaction. "You know I care about poor people, but he crossed the line."

"Yeah, he came into our space." Jake stood up. "I'm tired, sweetheart. I've got a lot going on tomorrow. Let's go."

CHAPTER 46

They drove from the diner to his condominium in silence. Jake did not understand why the scene in the diner had made him so uncomfortable. What the hell was the transgression? Was it about manners? Being civilized? When they arrived at his building, Jake kissed Becky good-bye and told her he would call later.

The doorman put the suitcases on a cart and took them upstairs. Jake followed him looking through his mail. When he unloaded the luggage, the doorman thanked Jake for his tip and left the room. Jake put his hat and the mail on the foyer table. He tossed his coat and jacket on a chair and then lay down on a couch and closed his eyes.

Jake dreamed that he was at the diner he had just left. He was wearing a tuxedo, when two couples, dressed in formalwear, invited him to go with them to a cotillion. As the five of them walked from the restaurant, only Jake appeared to care that the black boy, sitting alone, was neither invited nor even noticed by the others.

Outside Jake was leading a parade of people in gowns and tuxedoes. They marched around a beautiful room and then through the hotel where the slave museum gala was taking place. When they walked past the grand ballroom, Jake saw vice president Carver talking to president Simba and Hinda, and he quickly joined them.

The vice president whispered to Jake, "president Simba told me he has known you since you were a baby. Hinda said that she recently got to know you in the biblical sense of the word."

President Simba told Jake, "The vice president showed me the great monument to America's first president. She said the enormous white shaft is a reminder of what the western world did to Africa."

A telephone caller with the wrong number woke Jake from the dream.

CHAPTER 47

At Ruth's hospital room, Jake hesitated, knocked and then walked in when JM opened the door. He shook JM's hand and kissed Ruth.

"Don't look so sad Jakob," Ruth said. "They're going to keep me comfortable. They promised no pain. We found a beautiful place in Florida. It's the right thing for me and for everybody I love."

Jake was too moved to speak.

"Tell me about your trip," Ruth said

"My parents created a great country. It is named for them. They must have known they were going to die when they sent me away." He paused. "You don't seem surprised."

"Hinda called us after you met Yochevet," JM said. "She calls Ruth every day."

"What did you think of your people, their culture?" Ruth asked.

"I now understand why it was your second home," Jake said.

"And my Hinda, Nu, what did you think of her?" Ruth asked.

"I fell in love."

"So how does this story end?" Ruth asked.

"In a few months I could be an advisor to the president. It should make you proud."

"President of which country?" Ruth asked.

"Which country? Are you serious?"

Ruth was not happy with his answer. "Bessedelya is your birthplace. With your help, it could be a great nation, a model for all of Africa. You'd compare that to a presidential advisor? And Hinda, don't you see it was meant for you to be with her?"

Jake walked to the window. "I was told that our president has something in mind for me. He wants to see me this week. Hinda's a married woman."

"I feel nauseated," Ruth said. "Joshua, call my nurse, please. Jakob go. You'll be late for your meetings."

As he walked out of the hospital room, Jake looked at his two old friends, and his eyes filled with tears. He had never before considered life without Ruth and JM.

CHAPTER 48

Renowned financial experts had been called to the White House to discuss the worst global crisis since the Depression. After having listened to hours of sophisticated arguments, the best course of action was obvious to Jake and the other participants. To everyone's chagrin, they were told the president would pursue an ill-conceived short-term plan because it was the only one Congress would approve.

Jake recalled Hinda's comment in Davos. 'If your silence will be considered assent, vote with your feet.' He pushed his seat back from the table, stood up and left the room. No one had ever walked out of a meeting with this president of the United States.

Outside the building, reporters were quick to question the tall African American.

"Have you killed your chance for a presidential appointment?"

Jake did not stop to respond.

CHAPTER 49

The traffic on the way to the Maryland suburb was unusually heavy. Large homes were visible above the snow-covered walls around his daughter's gated community.

"Jake Warsaw," he said to the policeman at the guardhouse. "Johnson party, I'm Mrs. Johnson's father."

"May I see your ID?" he asked. He looked at Jake and the driver's license and then at a clipboard with a list of names before he activated the electrically controlled gate.

The many cars on the street forced him to park a block away from the mansion. He put his cell phone in a charger, took his top coat from the backseat and started to the house. Several guests were at the windows admiring the Christmas lights on the tennis court and swimming pool. Inside he gave his coat to the hatcheck man at the door.

His daughter and ex-wife blew kisses from across the crowded room. As he worked his way toward the den, several people patted him on the back. CNN had reported he was being considered for a presidential appointment.

A Developing Country

On a large TV, the football game had ended, and a helmetless player and the winning coach were being interviewed. The sound from the set was muffled by the loud talk of game watchers who had risen from their seats. A teenager picked up the remote and began changing channels. When he was distracted by a friend, he stopped on a news program.

Jake was looking through the glass doors of the wine refrigerator at the precious bottles when a man and woman greeted him. He looked up and noticed a picture of Africa on the television screen.

"I'm glad you'll be advising the president Mr. Warsaw," the woman said. "Our country wouldn't be in this financial mess if he had been listening to you or reading your op-ed articles."

"A lot of good people give him advice. Deciding whose advice to take is difficult," Jake said.

The picture of Africa on the TV telescoped down to a country on the east coast. Jake saw the caption on the screen, *Massacre in Bessedelya*. It was followed by a split screen. One half showed a smiling man identified as Vice President Ali Mohammed. The other half of the screen showed two covered bodies being carried on stretchers from a bomb scene. One of the bodies was a child, and that stretcher was followed by a small dog.

Jake pushed past the woman he was talking to, climbed over the couch and grabbed the remote from the teenager. The noise in the room drowned out most of the comments from the reporter. Jake heard, "..known for the great resort Fun City. There was never any terrorist activity until recently in this modern democratic country." The reporter began other news stories.

Jake was unable to find anything about Bessedelya on the other channels. He felt for his cell phone and realized he had left it in his car. He saw a phone on the wall in the kitchen, but to get there, he had to maneuver through the people filling trays of food and others dumping food into garbage bags. He took the knife-slashed wallet from his jacket, found the business card from Fred Glazer and dialed his number.

He heard Fred's voice. "Yes? Hello. Hello."

"Fred, it's Jake. Jake Warsaw."

"Oh, Jake. There's chaos here."

"The president," Jake asked. "Is he all right?"

"He has no idea what's going on."

"Hinda. How is she?"

"The people she was meeting with were killed," Fred said. "She wasn't hurt, but she's in shock. She's got to pull herself together and soon."

"What do you mean?"

"We need Hinda. A neighboring country has gone on full alert. Our army is preparing to act. Ethnic groups that have lived together are suddenly at each others' throats. She may be the only one who can bring the peace, but she's got to step up. There is no time to lose."

"She hates politics. She'll never.."

"If she knew you would help her, she might. You could persuade her. Get here as soon as you can. I hope it's not too late."

"Impossible. I'm supposed to meet the president in a few days."

"You're breaking up. Heard 'impossible.' There is nobody else." The phone went dead.

A Developing Country

Jake started to redial. He looked at the business card and then the cut wallet. As he put the phone in its cradle, he heard his name.

"Jake," his daughter called from the den. "Everybody wants to meet you. They said on TV that the Treasury secretary's name is on the dollar bill."

A server, trying to avoid him, spilled his dishes. Jake was reminded of the old lady who said, "Eedel," when she looked at him and saw his father's face. Jake apologized to the waiter and moved out of the way.

A dishwasher saw the crowd at the kitchen doorway calling to the tall man staring into space. "Man, don't just stand there, do something," he said, laughing.

He dialed his secretary's phone. "Kay," he said to her voice mail. "This is Jake. Cancel all my appointments. You can say it's a family matter."

CHAPTER 50

The next day, when Jake walked into his favorite restaurant, he saw JM standing up, holding his newspaper.

A waiter was blotting spilled coffee while a busboy began to change the tablecloth.

"We should eat at restaurants where they charge less for a dried piece of fish and the portions are larger," JM said.

"That would be any other restaurant in town," Jake said. He sat down, looked at the familiar menu and picked up his newspaper.

The waiter showed the plate of fish to Jake. "The schmaltz is running out of it. Can you imagine anyway to satisfy the old bastard?"

JM seemed to think about the question. "I want an America where a waiter respects learned men like Mr. Warsaw and me."

The waiter laughed, "Since you two bums began advising Washington, the country's gone down the shitter. Nine percent unemployment, the worst recession in eighty years and now, you and your Wall Street brothers grab bonuses and leave town. I say good riddance."

"We gave great advice," JM said. "It was too often ignored."

"What do you think, Mr. Warsaw?" the waiter asked.

Jake looked up from his paper. "Index funds. Stay invested in index funds."

"Maybe you didn't notice the market's down two hundred goddamn points."

Jake pointed to a fruit item on the menu. "Mr. Mitchell and I together have an enormous amount of wisdom. Who could possibly give you better advice?"

"My friend's son went to Wharton. He analyzed my stocks, bonds, 401k, real estate—the whole *megillah*. He said in his opinion I should try to find a rich wife." The waiter went to seat people at another table.

JM asked, "Are you leaving tonight?"

Jake nodded.

"I tried to talk Ruth into going to a hospice in Bessedelya," JM said. "Hinda told us the fighting is over, the country's back to normal and she's recovered. She pleaded with us to come. Ruth said she thinks we should be near the children."

"Did you tell Hinda I was coming?"

"No. You told us you wanted to surprise her."

The waiter brought Jake a plate of fruit and cottage cheese, filled their coffee cups and walked away.

"Everybody doesn't bounce right back from a colon operation," JM explained. "Sometimes type A guys like you go through a depression when they suddenly have to slow down."

"I'm getting a second opinion. They have antidepressants," Jake replied.

"The remediation of your farm is going to take a lot of your time and cost a fortune. It may be worse than the cancer. You know the neighbors will say you caused them to go bald and the environmental groups won't leave you alone."

"Are you trying to tell me that I shouldn't go to Bessedelya?"

"I don't know what the hell I'm saying. Ruth's condition, you're leaving, I'm not ready to deal with all this."

CHAPTER 51

Hinda's clothes were discolored from sweat when she walked into her house after her morning jog.

Lilah was standing at the sink cutting fruit and watching television. "You had a call from Jerusalem. Aaron's doctor wants to discuss his case. I wrote his number down."

Hinda took a piece of fruit, looked at the note, and walked to the bathroom where she dropped her clothes and went into the shower.

A short time later, there was a knock at the door.

"Tell Hinda General Nemonah would like to see her."

Lilah gave him a seat at the table, poured him some coffee and then went to the bathroom door. "General Nemonah's here to see you. I'm going to the store. Do you need anything?"

A few minutes after Lilah left, Hinda came out in her bathrobe.

General Nemonah said, "How are you feeling girl? Everybody's worried about you."

"Much better thanks, and thanks for the flowers," she said, pointing to several baskets around the room.

"I met with the president to discuss the terms of a peace treaty we've been offered. He didn't understand what I was talking about. Maybe this afternoon he won't be confused, but we need a leader now. Hinda, you're the only one everyone will follow."

"I'm flattered Joe, but I know I can't do the job. And I'm not sure the country can't run itself until we choose a new president and vice president. The bureaucracy works well. We have diplomats who can advise you on the treaty."

"You're talking like an idiot. You convinced us that we must have civilian control, but we need a decision maker, someone the people and the army will support.

"You don't want me. I would never have approved the way you killed so many civilians and then did so much damage to their electrical system and sewage treatment plants. What the hell were you thinking?"

"I wanted them to see what it will cost them to keep ignoring our warnings. Have you talked to the mothers who, when they hear the alarms go off, have fifteen seconds to find their children and get them into shelters? When you're president, explain to these families why we should keep trying to reason with people who've said they want to kill us."

As they talked, they noticed but ignored the tremor that shook the small house and rattled the glassware.

"We've known each other forever," he continued. "We'll never agree on many things, but Bessedelya needs a president. Appoint a strong chief of staff who knows how the country works. He'll do the administrative stuff that you hate. Your presence will reassure the people. I can tell you our enemies will soon test us. At least take the job until we have an election. Let me have some more coffee."

Hinda filled his cup and cut him a piece of cake. "A chief of staff? Sometimes you surprise me. I would want somebody who has the experience running a big organization. Someone I trust."

"I'm not available," Nemonah said.

"I think you're guilty of war crimes."

"Our response was justified by military necessity."

"Billy Gee."

"You know his brother was behind the terrorist attacks. His family fled the country. Pick anybody but BG."

"If you want me to take the job, tell BG to call me. Set up a meeting with our congressional leaders, the heads of our biggest industries, our most esteemed elders. I want to hear their priorities and objections. I want them to see how BG reacts to their concerns."

General Nemonah's phone rang. "Ahuva! The Science Institute. Was the hospital damaged? I'll call you in a few minutes. I'm on my way."

Nemonah made notes on a pad and then looked at Hinda. "The epicenter of the earthquake was at Ahuva, a lot of casualties."

"My son takes classes there. Wait, I'm going with you."

"You'll be in my way. Take your car," Nemonah said as he left the house.

Hinda got no answer from her calls to Stefen as she dressed. She was on her way out the door when the phone rang.

"What are you doing for supper?" It was Jake Warsaw.

"Jake is it you?"

"I'm at your airport."

"There's been an earthquake where Stefen goes to school. He's not answering his phone. As soon as I find out if he's all right, I'll meet you."

"Don't worry about me. Just tell me where you'll be, and I'll find you."

"No, wait at the baggage area. I'll pick you up. Jake, I'm so glad you're here."

Jake bought a newspaper and walked to the wall with the political advertisements. Ali and BG posters had not been removed since his last visit.

Downstairs at the arrival area, a BG Industry van stopped. A man jumped out and ran inside to the luggage carousel. He grabbed the only two suitcases on the moving belt and took them into the car. When Jake finally came and did not find his bags, he reported them missing and then walked outside to wait for Hinda.

CHAPTER 52

"**Where's your luggage?" Hinda asked** after a long kiss.

"When you're starting life over, you learn to make do with less. Have you heard from your son?"

"He just called. He's working with the rescuers. I don't see your suitcases."

"When they find them, they'll send them to the hotel."

The airport police waved to her to move her car.

A mile from the airport he said, "Pull over. I want to kiss you."

As she continued driving she reached for his hand. "I'm a little worried about Ruth. I left word on her answering machine."

"Ruth wasn't doing well, so JM decided to leave everything and get her settled at the hospice."

"Oh Jake, if they left that quickly, I'm sure she could use my help. I want to be with her."

"Whenever you're ready, we'll go."

"Thank you, sweetheart. I'll feel so much better if I can be with her. Tonight I'm going to make you very happy."

Jake laughed. "How will Stefen react to my being with you?"

"I don't know. He was a difficult kid before Aaron moved in. They'll both have to understand that I want to live with you. Now tell me about the presidential appointment."

"I won't be secretary of the Treasury."

"I'm sorry."

"I'm not. I thought it was important. I feel differently now."

Army trucks and cars with blinking lights rushed past them on the way to Ahuva. A few miles from that city, Hinda pulled into the parking lot in front of the largest of several one-story buildings. A sign read, Welcome to Shalom Park.

"Religious groups share these buildings," Hinda said. "Wait for me inside. I'll be back in ten minutes."

Jake walked past the information desk into a library as Hinda disappeared into a room down the hall. People in earphones sat in alcoves and others at tables were reading quietly. The bookshelves were marked with the names of many different spiritual practices. There were DVDs of various services. One section had meditation instructions and new-age music. Another had commentaries on the ceremonies and rituals of sects and tribes from all over the world.

Bulletin boards had contact information for ministers, priests and other holy men. Jake was reading the schedules of different services taking place when he heard a children's choir coming from outside the library. He walked down a hall and saw a chapel with six people listening to the choir while watching a religious service on a large screen.

From a room in the back, Hinda came into the hall dabbing her eyes. She grabbed Jake's hand and led him to the car.

"Do you come here often?" Jake asked.

"I've never been to this center before."

"Are you religious? I mean are you Islamic or Christian?"

"I go to all kinds of religious services," Hinda said. "I don't understand the Latin in the Catholic service or the Hebrew in the Jewish one, but I love them all. My boyfriend in America was embarrassed by spirituals and gospel singing, so I'd go to some churches by myself."

Jake didn't feel comfortable in religious discussions and was surprised by Hinda's enthusiasm. When pressed, Jake would say he believed in Intelligent Design or Deism, but now his colon tests results were on his mind every day. "Do you believe God hears your particular prayers?"

She smiled. "I believe God brought me from slavery to a promised land. That would have been enough, but he gave me Stefen and my wonderful life. That would have been enough. Now he's brought you to me. There have been too many miracles in my life to have just been coincidences. Besides, it makes me feel good to tell God how grateful I am."

CHAPTER 53

In a few minutes they arrived in Ahuva. It was a surreal scene. Part of the modern city was badly damaged, but many buildings appeared untouched by the earthquake. Hundreds of relief workers and military personnel were searching the rubble for survivors. Stretchers carried injured to ambulances and other vehicles bound for hospitals and emergency treatments.

Hinda and Jake entered a first aid station. They witnessed a young couple cursing a tall man with a stethoscope. When the couple finally left him, the doctor recognized Hinda and walked slowly to her.

"They were angry with me for how I told them about their baby. I'm a board-certified pediatrician who's been practicing for more than twenty-five years. I've never known how to tell parents terrible news about their children."

In another tent they visited, an oriental woman waved for Hinda to come to her.

"Professor Osaka, thank God you're all right," Hinda said as they hugged.

"I know you must be concerned about Stefen," Osaka said. "I saw him and Kim about an hour ago. They were carrying people to ambulances near their school. I told them to check in with me, but I haven't heard from them since then."

"I just talked to Stefen. They were getting ready to take a break," Hinda said. "Is your husband all right?"

"He's away at a seminar. I don't think he knows what's happened, but I left word for him not to worry about us."

"What can I do for you?"

"I can't get to my car," she said. "If you could get someone to take me home, I would be very grateful."

"We will be happy to take you. Mr. Warsaw is my friend from America."

"These two boxes, can you help me carry them?" the professor asked Jake.

"Professor Osaka's son Kim and Stefen have been friends since first grade," Hinda explained. "She teaches physics at the Science Institute and her husband teaches at the Divinity School."

"I teach mathematics," the professor corrected. "Dr. Osaka teaches philosophy."

Jake picked up the two cartons. They were filled with files, computer CDs and pictures.

Inside Hinda's car, Osaka covered her face and began crying. "My most brilliant student died to save these files. He kept going back to get more of his papers and the building collapsed. I begged him not to go."

"Why were they so important?" Jake asked.

"They represent years of work. He had a breakthrough on his research and was preparing to publish his findings. He was auditing my fractal geometry class to use more of Mandelbrot's work. It enabled him to get his arms around the enormous amount of data he was accumulating. He told me that now he could model complex systems in equations and translate them into patterns and pictures."

She took some pictures from one of the boxes. "These are called fractals. Using these pictures, he showed us relationships between different motions, for example, the transition from a relatively quiet state to the onset of turbulence. He introduced me to his friends as the lady who could describe the movement of water coming from a waterfall."

"Was his work worth dying for?" Jake asked.

"He realized its extraordinary importance when he was able to predict the time and place of the last two largest earthquakes. No one in the world has been able to do this. This morning he was telling us the places where the next two would be."

"But he didn't predict the one that killed him," Hinda said.

"His work only showed earthquakes above 8.9 on the Richter scale. The one today was less powerful. If your car CD works, you could listen to him and his last predictions."

CDs had been thrown into the cartons and were mixed with folders and charts.

"This one may be from this morning," she said as she handed a CD to Jake. "He was telling us the coordinates that indicate locations of the next two nine-plus earthquakes. The first one will hit within two weeks near Easter Island. The one after that was a city in Egypt, I think, and then there was the terrible roar that sounded like a train."

A Developing Country

The voice on the CD said, "Everyone looks at the porosity of the rock, the fault lines and the history. We looked at turbulence underground and assumed there is a steady accumulation of pressure. The only common discovery was that each of the components broke down to different scales, to smaller and smaller elements, and each was affected by many things."

The professor hit fast-forward.

"Faults and fractures crisscross the surface of the earth in three dimensions. These cracks control the flow of water, natural gas, oil. They control the behavior of earthquakes. Our fractal maps show gaps that allow fluids to flow and where pressures will build. The pressures show up like a wave and expose patterns of motion that are otherwise invisible."

When Hinda turned into a housing development, she ejected the CD and gave it to Jake to return to the box.

"I'm impressed that you remembered my neighborhood," the professor said. "I'm in the fourth house on the right. If I find the last CD and it seems important, I'll call you. Write your telephone number for me."

The professor hugged Hinda, and she thanked Jake after he carried the boxes into her house.

CHAPTER 54

A sign read **Welcome to Ahuva.** Hinda pointed to a modern building. "That's the research institute where Professor Osaka teaches." They drove past a crew trying to move a section of a building that lay on an exposed locker room. Finally, they saw Stefen and Kim. They were moving a child from a stretcher into an ambulance. When the boys saw Hinda, they walked to her as she parked the car.

After hugging them both Hinda said, "Kim I think your mother would like to hear that you're okay."

He took out his cell phone and walked away.

"You remember Jake?" Hinda asked Stefen.

They shook hands.

Jake said to Stefen, "How are you handling all this?"

Stefen shook his head. "Not well. I want to talk to Kim's father. He helped me understand why Aaron shut down after Rwanda."

"He's a good teacher?"

"I've sat in on some of his classes. It takes me a while to digest what I think I heard him say. A lot of times it's over my head."

"What do you think he might say about all this?"

"He told a class that whoever created this world must have had a plan, because there is an order to the universe. The closest we can get to understand that plan is our observations of nature. One day we may learn why he created mosquitoes or gravity.

"What did he say about natural disasters and all the suffering they cause?" Hinda asked.

"Hurricanes and floods are not good or evil. He doesn't understand why a God who would have created intelligent lives would then inflict so much pain on them, but it's foolish to think that our individual actions are punished or rewarded by the creator of the galaxies. The universe could not be organized around the brief lives of human beings."

Jake said, "Religions believe that because God is perfect, the world we live in would not be his second best work, something that can be improved or fixed."

Stefen looked at the devastation around them. "You mean this could be the best of all the possible worlds he could have created?"

Two tractors with excavator cranes on their trailers stopped near where they were talking. A crane operator, sitting next to the driver of one of the tractors, stepped out and drove both cranes, one at a time, off the trailers. The tractor trailers then left, and the operator drove one of the excavators toward a collapsed building.

He was followed by several people trying to get him to go in the opposite direction to a science laboratory. The roof of that small building had caved in, preventing the escape of several students.

With people screaming for anyone to help the trapped lab students and no apparent operator for the second crane, Jake climbed into its cab. The instrument panel and pedals were familiar. Many years ago, when he had worked at a port, the crane operators had let him play with the equipment when there was no one around. Jake climbed down from the crane aware of his inexperience and anxious to see someone who might be a qualified to do the job.

An old man pleaded, "The roof fell in the laboratory building. It's blocking the door. Please, mister, bring the crane. You just have to move the roof."

"I'll do my best," Jake said reluctantly," but try to find a crane operator."

Jake climbed into the cab and figured out how to turn the cab and move forward. After a few mistakes with the levers, he was able to control the "thumb" that held the load and to open and close the bucket.

Spectators impatiently witnessed his efforts to control the machine and begged him to hurry to the students' rescue. When no operator appeared, Jake started walking the crane the long distance to the laboratory.

A slab of concrete blocked his path. The crane rocked and jerked as he maneuvered the bucket to grab the concrete, swung it to the side and moved closer to the building. He raised the bucket, bit into a corner of the roof and slowly lifted that section. The crowd let out a shout when they saw seven people in the laboratory crawl out from under tables. The smiling survivors raised their hands with thumbs up. Stefen and Kim called to their friends to tell them to make their way through the debris to the door.

Suddenly there was a terrifying crunching noise as the bucket continued to bite through the shingles and joist beams. The roof slowly worked loose, fell in and again covered the laboratory. Jake tried to grab another section. There were screams from the spectators as they pointed to smoke and flames visible from the room.

A heavyset man pulled Jake out of his seat, and then skillfully grabbed the roof and swung it out of the way. Now standing alongside the crane, Jake saw that the scene in the laboratory was tragically different. The same students, recently smiling and waving, now lay lifeless in the smoke-filled room.

Jake and several men ran alongside Kim and Stefen through the rubble into the laboratory. The smoke burned his lungs as he tried to lift two people lying on the floor. Grabbing one with each hand, he pulled them to the doorway where others took them outside. He started to go back, but someone told him there were no more people in the room.

Still trembling with emotion and covered with ashes, Jake walked toward Hinda's car.

A priest patted him on his back. "You delivered God's message."

"What do you mean?" Jake asked.

"Those people were doing stem-cell research."

A woman shouted at Jake, "You killed those kids. If you didn't know what you were doing, you shouldn't have run the crane."

Hinda leaned out her car window. "Come Jake, let's go. Stefen and Kim are staying."

CHAPTER 55

When Jake and Hinda walked into the hotel, the staff greeted them with a hero's welcome. Looking at Jake's dirty clothes, the manager said, "We heard you were at Ahuva. I have good news. Your suitcases were found outside the airport. The men who took them were caught when they threw them on the road. We sent your clothes to be cleaned. They should be delivered soon."

When Jake and Hinda got off the elevator, they saw two teenagers undressing each other at the end of the hall. Laughing, they disappeared into a room.

Inside Jake's room, they found his opened suitcase, a bottle of tequila, a container of ice and a bowl of fruit. Jake went into the bathroom.

When Hinda answered her cell phone, she heard BG's voice on the speaker.

"General Nemonah told me to call you," BG said. "He asked if I would work as your chief of staff until the next election. I said I would discuss it with you."

"You can't be considered until you answer for John," Hinda said. "He did too much damage."

"I wouldn't consider coming back if I thought you had the slightest doubt about my involvement in any activity that would hurt anyone."

"I believe you, but it's not my decision. The judges do not want you to return because it would break precedent, and the people would say the law does not apply to the rich. The leaders want me to run the country until the next election, but I couldn't do the job for one week."

"You would be a great president."

"Our country needs an experienced manager. I'm not that person."

BG said, "As president, it's not your job to oversee the institutions. You set the standards. You will make our values clear to our people and to the world. The people will trust you to lead the country through this transition. A chief executive officer would do the day-to-day work."

"Some things can't be delegated," Hinda said. "There are continuous requests for our people and our resources, but we simply can't help everyone. I think I'm suffering from *compassion burnout*."

"You do sound exhausted, but I'm ready to help you. Just tell me what you want me to do."

"Explain to the decision makers why I would need a chief of staff. Persuade them to allow you to take charge. Convince them that you are totally committed to helping us get through this crisis. I don't want this job, but I'm afraid our country could be in serious trouble without our help."

"You know I wouldn't come back without my wife and children, and I'd like you to at least try to let my parents return." BG said. "If you can make that happen, I will do anything the courts ask of me."

"And what about the court of public opinion?"

"Give me time to work with you. After several months, the people should vote on my performance. If they want me and my family to leave the country, we'll go. In any event, we will continue to make restitution for John's actions until we've fulfilled our obligations."

"You will be meeting with the decision makers," Hinda said. "Considering their ages and attention spans, you won't have much time to explain why they should trust us to bring our country out of this crisis."

"We'll do the best we can," BG said and hung up.

Hinda put her cell phone on the nightstand and said, "I've got a change of clothes in my car. I'll be back in a few minutes."

As she left, the cleaners came with his clothes. Jake was hanging them in the closet when Hinda's cell phone rang. It was Professor Osaka.

"Dr. Raisal?" Osaka said. "Oh Mr. Warsaw. I just heard the CD with my student's last comments. He reminded us that there will be hundreds of earthquakes around the world during the next several months. He said we cannot know which will be the most destructive, but he can say where and when the largest eruptions will take place."

Hinda returned to the room and heard Osaka on the speaker of her cell phone.

"Less than two weeks from now, thirty miles north northeast of Easter Island, there will be a 9.1 earthquake. I misunderstood where he said one would hit eighty days later. Just as the roar started, I heard him say Alexandria. I thought

A Developing Country

he was talking about Egypt, but when I replayed it just now, it was clear he said Alexandria, Virginia."

Jake looked at Hinda and said, "Dr. Osaka, Alexandria is south of Washington, DC. We must share this information with officials in America as soon as possible. They will want to analyze the data that led to his conclusions. May I arrange to send someone to pick up the files and CDs he gave you? Thank you. If you could provide the contact information for any of his associates familiar with his work, it would be helpful."

Even before Jake hung up, Hinda was on the hotel phone with someone and gave him Dr. Osaka's home address and phone number. She told him to make copies of everything in the two cartons, pack them in envelopes and bring them to the hotel.

As soon as Jake said good-bye to Osaka, he called his secretary in America.

A voice with a southern accent said, "This is Patti Lancaster, Mr. Warsaw. Kay is not well. She said if you need her to call her at home. She gave me a file that has your calendar, how to contact key people you talk with, travel instructions and other information that she takes care of for you."

Jake remembered Kay's enthusiastic recommendation of Lancaster with one exception, because of Patti's Alabama drawl, she was often asked to repeat herself.

"Are you ready to take some notes?" Jake asked.

"Yes sir."

"Call Joshua Mitchell. Tell him to set up a meeting for me, as soon as possible, with the president of the United States or the vice president. The meeting should include a mathematician who can explain fractal geometry and chaos theory. There should be an expert in earthquakes. Prepare a brief description of the latest earthquake research. If any of the papers seems particularly interesting, see if the authors will be available for the meeting with the president. Am I going too fast, Ms. Lancaster?"

"No, sir."

"Good. Tell Mr. Mitchell the White House should invite someone from the Defense Department, Transportation Department, Treasury Department and Homeland Security to this meeting.

"Before or after that meeting I want to visit the hospice where Mr. Mitchell's wife is staying. Ask him to suggest a hotel. I will be traveling to and from Bessedelya to every meeting with Dr. Hinda Raisal."

"Will you want one or two hotel rooms and will you want a car with a GPS?" Lancaster asked.

"One room and yes."

Hinda touched Jake's shoulder. "Stefen could use a break. Can we take him? Ruth would love to see him, and he might want to see what an American university looks like."

Jake said to Lancaster, "Add a plane ticket for Dr. Raisal's son, Stefen. Try to arrange meetings with admission officers at the best colleges. Get him a driver or escort. He's never been to the states before. If you can't arrange the meetings for him, get him a separate room at our hotel."

"I'll need some other information about Dr. Raisal and her son, if they are not American citizens."

Hinda took the phone, answered Patti's other questions, and then gave the phone to Jake.

"Call me as soon as you have any information," Jake said before he hung up.

Hinda put her arms around Jake. "I need some information. Do you think we could snuggle while I ask you some questions?"

"Can you wait until after I shower?"

"No."

CHAPTER 56

Four hours later Jake's cell phone rang. It was Patti Lancaster.

"Mr. Warsaw, you have three tickets on a flight that stops in Rome and then goes to Dulles with a two-hour layover before you and Dr. Raisal leave for Florida.

"After your arrival in Florida, you have a meeting at your hotel with a geologist who's now an administrator with Norfolk State College. He wrote what I thought was a simplistic idea about reducing the impact of an earthquake by changing the trajectory of its forces at the epicenter. He agreed to fly down to Florida and to wait at the hotel until you can see him. I got him rooms at your hotel and in Washington and a ticket on your plane, if you want him to go with you.

"The president will be unavailable. The vice president will send her administrative assistant, some scientific advisors and representatives from the cabinet secretaries. My impression, from talking to the people suggested by Mr. Mitchell, was that both the president and the vice president were unwilling to meet with you because of something you did or did not do.

"I could not find a dependable escort for Stefen Raisal, so I've arranged for him to go from Dulles to New York with me. We have appointments at NYU and Columbia. The next day, we'll go to Johns Hopkins in Baltimore and then meet you at Dulles for your return home.

"If these arrangements are okay, I'll send you the information about your Washington meeting, Florida hotel, car confirmations and a backgrounder on the geologist. If I get anything else, I'll bring it when I meet you at Dulles."

"Ms. Lancaster," Jake said, "My budget is not unlimited. If instead of separate rooms for you and Stefen you get one room with one bed, there could be substantial savings."

"I have a boyfriend, Mr. Warsaw."

"You did a good job. Thank you, Ms. Lancaster."

CHAPTER 57

As they landed in the United States, Hinda showed Jake an e-mail from the journalist Fred Glazer. He said president Simba was shocked to learn that BG's father, William, was invited to take over the country. He insisted on attending the meeting when his old friend will be interviewed. He was especially hurt that Hinda had stolen money from his bank account to use for her trips. Glazer wrote that so far, the media agreed not to report these stories.

CHAPTER 58

Jake and Hinda were met at Dulles by a blonde twenty-one-year-old Patti Lancaster carrying a sign that read Jakob Warsaw. After a brief greeting she told them that in order for Stefen and her to make their plane to New York, they would have to hurry to get to another terminal and then through security. Stefen grabbed the suitcases and followed Patti.

Patti was surprised by her discomfort as people turned to look at the tall, handsome black man running with her to the shuttle bus that would take them to their gate. When they got in the security line, she positioned herself behind Stefen and discouraged any conversation with him.

Once they were seated on the plane, she turned away from him until they were airborne. Stefen, confused by Patti's actions, fell asleep. When the stewardess offered a drink to Patti, he awoke and asked for coffee.

"This article I'm reading is very disturbing," Patti said, putting down her magazine. "What do you do about poverty in Bessedelya?"

"When a boy and girl first meet in my country, they don't usually begin talking about such a heavy subject," Stefan laughed.

"I'm a little uncomfortable," Patti admitted.

"Did I say something wrong?"

"I've been rude. I didn't want it to look like we're together." Patti began to blush.

"Your face turned red. Are you okay?"

Patti nodded.

"Everyday, people come to our country with different skin colors and strange customs. Almost immediately the young people make friends. It takes the older immigrants longer to get comfortable, but Bessedelya's people make everyone feel welcome."

"How would they feel about someone like me?" Patti asked.

Stefen looked serious. "Good news and bad news. The bad news for you is that in my country, black is beautiful. Your hue is not popular. The good news is some people practice polygamy and would like to have a white lady in their family. Some very old men who cannot get a black girlfriend might settle for a white woman if she's not too skinny."

Patti did not know if he was joking. "I wasn't planning to move there anytime soon."

"To your question about poverty," Stefen said, "I don't think we have any. Nobody goes hungry. Everyone gets health care and free education. We have almost no unemployment or homeless. If people have mental problems but can live by themselves with some assistance, we provide them homes or shelters."

A Developing Country

Patti had become attracted to this poised and articulate young man. She decided to show Stefen that she could discuss sensitive subjects. "Shelters for homeless people can be dangerous for women and young people. When I was fifteen, my father and I were homeless after a hurricane killed my mom and ruined our house. One night, three boys attacked me in the laundry room. When my dad came to try to help me, they shot and almost killed him."

"That's a terrible story. I'm really sorry," he said. "In Bessedelya, anyone who commits a violent act is put to death, and his entire family is banished from the country. We believe if a person knows he will certainly die, he will think twice before hurting someone. Rape is almost nonexistent. We know it's human nature to have sexual desires, so we have state-controlled safe places where any boy or girl can have a private sexual experience anytime they want."

Patti put down her magazine and said, "Mr. Warsaw told me that there were budget limitations on our trip. If we had to share a room at the hotel, would you be upset?"

CHAPTER 59

As soon as **Hinda and** Jake arrived at their hotel in Florida, Hinda called JM.

"Ruth is asleep," JM said. "I'll call you when she wakes up. I know she'll be excited to see you both."

As Jake was checking in, Hinda walked over to the one black man sitting in the lobby reading a magazine.

"I'm Dr. Hinda Raisal. Are you waiting for Jakob Warsaw?"

"Yes I am," he said standing and removing his hat. "My name is James Shenton."

"We appreciate your coming to meet with us. Let's move to a table where we can talk."

They went to a corner of the lobby by the coffee shop and sat in the restaurant's wicker chairs. Jake came to the table followed by a waitress. After greeting Dr. Shenton, Jake said, "We're starved. Let's get something. We may be interrupted by a call from a hospital. If we have to leave, we will return as soon as possible. Is that okay with you?"

A Developing Country

After they ordered food, they discussed their respective backgrounds and his doctorate in geology.

Shenton said, "When Ms. Lancaster called, I admit I hadn't thought about my article since graduate school. Considering today's scientific advances, my work was primitive. It was based on the premise that one day we would be able to predict where and when an earthquake would strike. If that were possible, we might be able to redirect the tremendous forces that come from the epicenter. This might be accomplished if we could open a path away from the earthquake that would relieve the shockwaves at the moment of their maximum force. To accomplish this, we would have to know the substrata, the hydrology and other geological information.

Jake asked, "Are you familiar with the geology around Washington DC?"

"Yes I am."

"If you knew that an earthquake with the power of nine on the Richter scale were going to strike Alexandria in two months, could you suggest a plan that would reduce the destruction of Washington?"

Dr. Shenton stood up and walked to a couch by the window. After about ten minutes, he took a paper placemat from a table, drew something on the back and handed Jake a sketch of a map. It showed a line from Alexandria that moved south for a few miles and then moved west southwest to Charlottesville.

After studying the drawing, Hinda said, "I assume your map is not the only way to save Washington and that you could determine different locations for the explosions."

"Yes," Shenton said.

"Then, in my opinion, this map is more about political science than geology," Hinda said.

"What makes you say that?" Jake asked.

"I assume nuclear explosives would be required to create the paths that would divert the enormous forces at the epicenter. Is that correct, Dr. Shenton?"

"Yes."

"If placed where Dr. Shenton has suggested, Washington might be saved, but the resulting radioactivity would make the land no longer inhabitable," Hinda said.

Jake said, "He's giving us a concept. If our scientists think other locations will work, they can choose a less destructive more cost-effective route. What is your objection to Dr. Shenton's placement of explosives?"

"His plan would destroy Monticello, Montpelier, and Mount Vernon three of America's most famous landmarks."

"How did you know that?" asked Jake.

"I spent a lot of time with the Founders of this country. My teachers thought the Federalist Papers were among mankind's most extraordinary accomplishments. But some of these great men were slaveholders. With Dr. Shenton's plan, nobody would ever again visit the homes of Washington, Madison or Jefferson."

Dr. Shenton looked down at the floor. "When I got my PhD in geology, I could not get a job at any of our best Virginia colleges including Mr. Jefferson's university. The only way I could feed my family was to take two jobs one in administration and one in the maintenance department.

"I watched thousands of black boys and girls handed a degree from a *separate but equal* school, knowing they had not been given the education white students received. I hated the adulation given the founders who had slaves. I had to use history books that ignored their despicable actions, breaking up families and selling women and children. My grandchildren, who attended Ivy League colleges, criticize me for being an angry black man. I'm afraid I'm too old to change."

Jake got a call from JM, who said if they could come now, Ruth was up and would be happy to see them.

Jake said, "Dr. Shenton, I hope you will join us tomorrow for our meeting at the White House. If your advice helps save the Capital, all the history books in the future will be rewritten with your contribution and your grandchildren will be more understanding."

CHAPTER 60

JM was waiting at the entrance of the hospice. He was shaking with rage. "Ruth was gasping for breath. I ran down the hall and got the doctor on duty. After he checked her, he told me there was nothing he could do. He said she was getting the medicines prescribed. I asked if there were any other procedures to help her breathe. He shook his head. I asked if he would adjust her morphine. He said he couldn't. Finally I asked him, if it were his wife or daughter would you? He said,'Do you want me to kill her?'"

JM sat down on a bench. "Just before you came, the shift changed and another doctor came on duty. When I told him how she was struggling, he made some adjustment and she dozed off."

"Should we come back later?" Jake asked.

"A nurse is with her now. When she comes out, we'll go in. She'll love to see you."

"Are your children here?" Hinda asked.

"My son's being honored by his favorite organization Ducks Unlimited, and my daughter sent a card."

After the nurse came out and spoke to JM, he waved for them to go in.

Hinda tried to hide her shock at the change in Ruth's appearance since she last saw her. Unable to restrain her tears, she kissed her special friend and said, "What a beautiful gown."

"You don't think it's too revealing? Darling, what is that bulge around your stomach? Do you have something you want to tell me?"

Hinda laughed. "You don't miss a thing. We heard the rabbit died. I thought Jake was fixed, and he thought I was on the pill."

"Mazel tov," Ruth said. "Jakob, now tell me what the doctor said about your colon tests."

"He told me a good percentage of his patients have had a complete recovery, but in my case, he'd like me to pay my bill before I leave his office."

"Did you both know the results and not tell me?" Ruth asked Hinda and JM.

"I didn't tell any of you," Jake said, "because I don't want you to spoil my plan."

"What the hell are you talking about?" JM asked.

"When I croak," Jake said, "I suspect many would come to the funeral home, sign the book but not stay to hear what a wonderful person I was. I will have my gloved hand sticking through a hole in my closed coffin. A photographer will take a picture of each person shaking that hand, otherwise they will not receive a personally signed *thanks for coming* letter from me and a CD of the eulogy."

Ruth smiled, "Give me another kiss and wait outside. I've got to nap for a few minutes."

In the hall, Jake told JM the reason for the meeting at the White House.

"If your information gets the two parties to finally cooperate," JM said, "you may have done more than save Washington."

CHAPTER 61

At the Capital, Hinda and Jake provided the assembled group of experts the little information they had, and then they were ushered into the administrative assistant's office.

An hour later, an angry Mort Plant arrived. "You are a real piece of work Mr. Warsaw. You embarrassed the vice president by the way you rejected her nomination of you to the cabinet. Now you repay her endorsement by giving her a problem that will hurt her however she handles it."

"Who should I have given the problem to?" Jake asked.

"Let me see if I understand the information you've brought," the AA began. "We may have to relocate millions of people away from Washington during the next eight or ten weeks. Our museums may have to have their treasures packed up and moved. Hundreds of thousands of government employees must find shelters and workplaces away from the city.

"All of this because a catastrophic event was predicted by a kid from India who never published a single paper, and he is not available to discuss his comments on the CDs because he is dead. We do not know how many of his predictions were accurate or if they happened at all.

"If he did predict where the epicenter would be, it would be an extraordinary accomplishment worth a Nobel Prize even if he were off by only thirty miles. But if he's off thirty miles, the DC earthquake could be Baltimore's problem not ours.

"I couldn't believe you brought us Dr. Shenton's half-assed plan. The man's an administrator at a little college for Christ's sake. I think he wants to take out Monticello and the University of Virginia to avenge Jefferson screwing Sally Hemmings.

"So what do we advise the vice president when she asks, 'How do we prevent a panic tomorrow when the media gets the story?' And how do we conduct government business when the staffs leave town? Maybe you have one more brilliant idea to share."

Jake didn't smile. "Congress could pass a bill that says, before the earthquake causes chaos, everyone must turn in their guns. The NRA will get the bill amended to say no earthquake will be permitted to hit Washington."

CHAPTER 62

As they walked into the airport terminal, Hinda and Jake were relieved that the highly emotional visit with Ruth and the intense discussions at the White House were behind them. They were talking about finding a bar when they saw Stefen and Patti's taxi arrive. Both were surprised to see Patti kiss Stefen after he paid the driver and picked up their luggage. Both were smiling as they approached Hinda.

Stefen began to tell Hinda how much he enjoyed New York and said, "Instead of going back with you, I'd like to stay a few more days. I could visit Ruth and Mr. Mitchell and look at a few more schools."

Before Hinda could answer Jake said, "I'm sure they would love to see you."

Hinda, still in shock from having seen them kiss said, "It would make Ruth happy."

"We'll get our tickets changed and meet you by that newsstand," Stefen said.

As they walked away holding hands Jake said, "I hope he watched your condom show."

Before their plane left for Africa, Hinda called the judge. She described the president's irrational behavior and the situation when Woodrow Wilson was incapacitated. The judge assured her that the now incompetent president would be restrained and not interfere in the transition to a temporary government and then asked," Who was Woodrow Wilson?"

CHAPTER 63

A few hours after they arrived in Bessedelya, BG's interview was about to take place in the auditorium of a school near the airport. Hinda told BG to wait outside until after she and Jake greeted the country's leaders. When they entered the room, Hinda and Jake received a standing ovation.

Hinda began, "I am told that our countrymen want me to be an interim president. I am humbled by their confidence in me, but I do not have the ability to do the job alone.

"We were fortunate during the past year to have had Ali run the country as the president's health failed. For me to serve, I will require a chief of staff who can work with our excellent agencies and institutions. Billy Gee can ably fill that critical function until we elect a president and a new team.

"All of us know him as an exemplary businessman and as one of our most generous philanthropists. You should know that he and I disagree on many issues, but I have no doubt about his integrity, intelligence and love of our country. He is waiting outside to be questioned by you."

Someone asked, "On what issues do you disagree?"

"I am comfortable with the status quo. He would convene a constitutional convention. He would propose changing from direct voting by the people on all major issues to a proportional representation system with political parties. He wants to make it easier to replace ineffective bureaucrats and poor judges. He believes our country must be more involved with other nations. He does not believe in capital punishment. Other than these few minor issues, we have no disagreements."

Everyone laughed.

"Don't you see a governance problem?" asked a well-known businessman.

"I completely trust BG," Hinda said. "I think we are fortunate that he is willing to serve. I have no doubt that he will be an excellent manager of the people's business. I am leaving now. I want to visit Ahuva and then President Simba. His health continues to deteriorate. Keep him in your prayers. Now I must go."

Jake asked her, "Do you want me to go with you?"

"Stay and explain that BG and I will need their patience and support," Hinda said. "I'll meet you at the president's house. He'll be glad to see you. I should be there in half an hour."

BG entered the room, greeted everyone and said, "I accept full responsibility for my brother's crimes. My family was horrified by his actions. There should be an independent review of everything that happened. I pledge my family's entire fortune to help all those harmed. I would serve at the pleasure of Hinda and the Congress and not one day more. After a few months, you and the public should vote whether or not they want me to continue."

"We know you can manage," someone in the crowd said, "but Hinda told us that you two have fundamental disagreements about policy. Do you think Hinda would be a good president?"

"No. I think she will be a great president," BG said. "It is her vision that Bessedelya will lead the unification of all of Africa. Only then, she believes, will we realize our destiny to become one of the world's superpowers.

Jake had had such discussions with Hinda and was not surprised that she had shared her vision with BG. As he walked to the back of the room, BG's driver approached Jake and said, "Mr. Gee told me to take you wherever you want to go."

In the car, Jake picked up a newspaper lying on the seat. He scanned the pages until he noticed the headline, "Tsunami from Major Earthquake Devastates Easter Island."

CHAPTER 64

At the president's house, Jake walked through the unattended open front gate. He saw two people inside the small guard house, knocked on the door and a young girl came out.

"Are you the guard?" Jake asked.

"Yes sir," she said.

"I'm supposed to meet Dr. Raisal here and then the president," Jake explained.

"I don't know that person, but a lady came here about ten minutes ago. She was driving that," she said pointing to Hinda's car.

"Are you guarding the president?"

"Not really, mostly we help him if he calls us."

"Is that what those earphones are for?"

"No sir. We were listening to music."

A Developing Country

Jake knocked at the front door. It was unlocked. When he entered the foyer he saw Hinda cleaning a wound on Rachel's head. The president lay on the floor covered with blood. He was not moving.

Rachel was crying, "He accused me of stealing, and then he got a gun. Hinda tried to take it from him."

"Carry her to my car," said Hinda. "There's a hospital not far from here. I'll wait for the police."

Jake recalled Mkeeba's reaction to seeing blood on the president. "You could be killed before you have a chance to explain. The country needs you. Take Rachel. I'll wait here."

Hinda started to protest, but Jake said, "Don't argue with me."

They put Rachel in the car, and Hinda drove out of the compound.

Jake went to the guard shack, saw that the two lovers were busy and headed back to the president's residence.

CHAPTER 65

Jake walked past the president's body into a room with a few pieces of furniture. A blanket, a TV remote and a small pillow lay on an old sofa. He picked up the blanket and walked around the room intrigued by the hundreds of unframed photographs tacked to the walls.

He assumed there would be pictures of famous visitors and remarkable events, but no faces or places were familiar. There were people showing off their babies, boys and girls in caps and gowns in front of relatives and friends, children at play on beaches, and one family surrounded by pets, but most of the photographs were simply of smiling people. The president was in a few pictures, posing with a school baseball team, with a boxer and in a crouch alongside some sprinters at a track meet. There were no awards or citations or honorary degrees among the pictures, and no one was wearing a military uniform.

As Jake covered the president with the blanket, his phone rang. It was Kay. "Mr. Mitchell asked me to tell you that Ruth will probably not last the night. If so the funeral will be

Monday, and they will receive visitors at his house for the next few days."

Jake went into the kitchen. He put a teabag in a cup, filled the tea kettle and turned on the stove. He heard Hinda call his name.

"I'm in here," said Jake. "Would you like some tea?"

Hinda came in, sat down and said, "The judge is sending an undertaker for the president. Fred Glazer is writing the obituary and a news release for the wire services. I told them the burial will be Thursday. A memorial service next week will give time for the heads of state to arrange their schedules."

"JM left word that Ruth may die tonight," Jake said as he poured some tea.

Hinda covered her eyes. "I will miss her so much."

"Her funeral would be Monday. Should I get you a ticket? I'll be staying for a few days. You could be back here Wednesday to help with the arrangements." Hinda nodded. "Should I get a ticket for your new daughter-in-law?"

"Just Stephen please."

CHAPTER 66

Two days later they were in Richmond. JM's house was crowded with family and friends when Hinda and Jake arrived. Jake put their coats on a bed upstairs. When he came down, he greeted his daughter and Nancy and several associates from the firm. Hinda was talking to JM.

"He'd like us to be with the vice president until he can get away," Hinda said as JM turned to greet someone. "She's in the game room."

An unsmiling bodyguard was at the door. With the vice president's approval, they were allowed to enter. A guard who was inside left the room.

"I'm sorry about your president," the vice president said to Hinda. "You may be surprised to learn that although he did not meet with world leaders or attend international conferences, he and your country were widely admired. Our advisors told us that Bessedelya's culture could not be replicated anywhere else." She looked at Jake. "I understand that you recently came back from your first trip there. Did you find anything especially interesting?"

A Developing Country

"Too much to simply describe. The way they deal with violence and hate crime, their view of sexual behavior, the enormous turnout to vote on important issues. When you have time, I'd like to tell you about some of the things they're doing. " Jake then asked," Can you tell me what we are doing to prepare for the earthquake?"

The vice president said,"The information you brought was validated by our scientists. The Easter Island event confirmed the prediction. Planners are considering a suggestion to move the Capital to a mid-west state. Many agencies are tasked with the evacuation of the city and the surrounding area."

"How do they protect the documents that can't be moved in time?"

"Some are talking about an Israeli invention. They designed a desk for school children to hide under that protects them from rocket attacks. Of course, we are building much heavier models for our artifacts."

"What was the reaction to Dr. Shenton's plan?"

"A non-starter."

"Not feasible?"

"No political support."

"To save the Capital?"

"To save a black city that always votes Democratic."

When JM came in, Jake said, "Hinda has a plane to catch. We should go. If I drive, I'll be back in an hour. She wants to drive, says I'm too slow."

"If you let her drive, you will definitely be back much sooner," said JM. "Ruth says that Hinda's driving helps her remember all the prayers she knew as a child."

CHAPTER 67

At the doctor's office the next morning, Jake heard his colon test results and the suggested protocol. "The early diagnosis was important," the doctor said. "Thirty five percent of my patients have done well with the treatments I'll prescribe. We can discuss alternatives."

"I've read of some promising work being done in Germany and Mexico," Jake said.

"Contact the writers. Have them call me to explain their work. You can decide if it's better than what we're doing."

"I assume I may lose my hair. Are there other side effects?"

"There is one that I suggest you discuss with your wife or lady friends. You will be impotent for quite a while."

Jake tried to imagine who and when he would tell anyone about this news.

As he got in his car, Hinda called. "It was a terrible flight. I'm home, and the phone won't stop. I was just told that Nigeria is ready to agree to tangible trade agreements. If we bring together the economic community of West Africa, it could be the last major piece."

Jake laughed, "You still don't seem to understand that a united Africa can't be done."

"I have to stop talking about Africa's destiny," Hinda said. "The leaders obviously have different priorities. One of them told me his only concern was where the Capital would be located. Others question how their country would have fair representation when there is such a disparity in populations and resources.

"I'm sorry to tell you Jake Warsaw, because I love you, but you are stupid. When you came back, I told you we were going to make it happen.

"Stephen told me he is joining you at the airport. Email me your ETA. I'll pick you up."

"No. You'll worry if we run late."

"OK. I've got to take this call."

CHAPTER 68

At the airport terminal, **Stephen** and Jake finished eating. "Did you decide on a college?" Jake asked.

"None of the ones I visited. I don't think I'm prepared for your universities."

"We have great small schools."

"Patti took me to a couple of mostly black colleges. The students were very friendly. They showed me beautiful campuses with facilities for every kind of sport. When I asked about their academic programs, they had much less to talk about. None of our colleges have such big athletic programs, and all have more hours of study and mentoring. I know I'm going to need that help. If I had to choose right now, I'd say I'll do better back home. Now can I ask you a very personal question?"

"Anything," said Jake.

"You've known the world's most powerful leaders. Our country will never be as great as America. You have a chance for a presidential appointment. Why even consider a move to Bessedelya?"

"Hinda. I've never met anyone like her."

"What concerns me is that you're pretty old. If there's no more interest in sex or traveling, what happens to the relationship?"

"No problem, Jake laughed. "If she feels that way, I'll dump her and get another babe."

Stephen looked at his ticket. "Before I forget, I want to change my seat."

He took his backpack and went to the ticket counter. Two men, who had just checked in overheard Stephen mention Bessedelya.

"Excuse me son," said one of the men. "We're on our way to your country, actually Fun City. It looks so modern, could you explain why it's called a developing country?"

Jake paid the check at the restaurant, went back to his table and opened a magazine. His phone rang.

"Jake this is BG. It's about Hinda. She was driving with her husband and his caretaker. According to Lilah, Hinda was on her phone and screamed with laughter. Aaron panicked and did something that caused her to lose control of the car. She's in intensive care. I'll call you as soon as I get more information."

Stephen and the men interested in Bessedelya were laughing when Jake interrupted them.

FINI

Printed in the United States
By Bookmasters